NO SLAM DUNK

NO
SLAM
DUNK

MIKE LUPICA

Philomel Books

PHILOMEL BOOKS
an imprint of Penguin Random House LLC
375 Hudson Street
New York, NY 10014

Philomel Books is a registered trademark of Penguin Random House LLC.
Library of Congress Cataloging-in-Publication Data
Names: Lupica, Mike, author.
Title: No slam dunk / Mike Lupica.
Description: New York, NY : Philomel, 2018.
Summary: In Annapolis, Maryland, seventh-grader Wes is a good teammate
but this basketball season has been challenging because of his ball hog
teammate Dinero, who is determined to steal the spotlight, and Wes's army
veteran father, who is suffering from PTSD.
Identifiers: LCCN 2018006767 | ISBN 9780525514855 (hardback) |
ISBN 9780525514862 (ebook)
Subjects: | CYAC: Basketball—Fiction. | Veterans—Fiction. | Post-traumatic
stress disorder—Fiction. | Fathers—Fiction. | BISAC: JUVENILE FICTION
/ Sports & Recreation / Basketball. | JUVENILE FICTION / Social Issues /
Friendship. | JUVENILE FICTION / Family / Parents.
Classification: LCC PZ7.L97914 No 2018 | DDC [Fic]—dc23
LC record available at https://lccn.loc.gov/2018006767
Printed in the United States of America.
ISBN 9780525514855
1 3 5 7 9 10 8 6 4 2
Edited by Michael Green.
Text set in Life BT.

This book is for Taylor McKelvy Lupica,
for whom the song remains the same.
She walked into the room and changed everything.

ONE

EVERYBODY ALWAYS SAYS THERE'S ONLY one ball in basketball.

Now one had just hit Wes in the side of the face, making him feel like somebody had slapped him.

Hard.

It was a basic three-on-two drill: Wes on the right wing; Emmanuel Pike over on the left; Dinero Rey, the one leading the break, in the middle. There were two defenders waiting for them as they crossed half-court, waiting for Dinero to make the first move, to decide whether to keep the ball or pass it.

It was less than an hour into the Annapolis Hawks' first practice together. Wes was now Dinero's teammate, a year after they'd been the stars of opposing teams in the sixth grade. As Dinero made his way down the court, Wes knew the defenders were expecting him to give it up.

They knew what Wes did: Dinero was even better passing a basketball than he was dribbling it with either hand or shooting it from the outside or driving it to the basket. There was a reason why he was called Dinero even though his real name was Danilo.

He was money.

He was the smallest kid on the court. But that didn't matter. He was fast and smart and flashy, with a game as big as his smile. A lot of kids his age could shoot and handle and blow past you if you gave them an opening. But it was what he could do with the ball that set him apart, Wes knew, from other kids their age, not just in their town, Annapolis, but maybe northern Virginia, too, and from all the slick ballers in Washington, D.C. Even though Dinero was only twelve, you could look him up on YouTube and see for yourself.

Now the first pass Dinero threw his way, very first one, had hit Wes flush in the side of the face.

Wes knew it was nobody's fault but his own.

"When you don't pay attention," his dad had always told him, "what you generally do is pay."

Dinero Rey had basically told him the same thing before they started the drill. Be ready if you're open, he'd said.

"I might not be looking at you," Dinero said, "but you better be looking at me."

Then he'd given him a quick high five and that smile.

"We're gonna do big things, you and me," Dinero said. "Just you watch."

Then Wes hadn't been watching, and the ball caught him right next to his ear, bouncing off his hard head and out of bounds. The drill came to a stop in that moment, even though the ball kept rolling.

Wes could feel the heat of where the ball caught him, could almost feel the *impression* of the ball, on a night when he was no different from everybody else on the court at the new Annapolis Rec Center, and wanted to make the best possible impression, on his teammates, on his coach, everybody.

With his pale skin, Wes knew his face had to be getting red, and not just because of the ball hitting him, but the humiliation he was feeling.

Dinero got to him first.

"Sorry, dude," he said. "I thought for sure you were looking." He grinned, which only made Wes feel worse.

"My fault," Wes said.

"You okay?" The grin was still there.

"Yes."

No! Wes thought.

Anybody who'd ever seen Wes play, who'd seen the magic in his own game, always talked about what a great head for basketball he had.

Only he wasn't supposed to use it like this.

Not on the first day of practice with the rest of the Annapolis Hawks, an elite team of seventh-graders that, in a year, would be playing in a new elite league. The other seventh-graders, the ones who hadn't made the Hawks, would play in the same travel league in which they'd played last season. But the Hawks, they were moving on. And moving up.

There were other stars from last year's teams. But the two biggest were Dinero and Wes: the point guard and small forward who played big. The two guys who were going to do big things together.

What had he been thinking about while the ball was busy finding his face?

His dad.

But mostly how he needed this team as much as he'd ever needed anything in his life.

TWO

THE DREAM FOR THEIR FAMILY had always been that they would move back to Annapolis, where Wes's dad had graduated from the United States Naval Academy before he became a Navy SEAL.

And that is what they'd finally done, at the start of sixth grade for Wes Davies, as his dad was about to set off on one last mission with the SEALs, in Afghanistan.

Wes could still remember the day he and his mom had said good-bye to Lieutenant Michael Davies. To Wes, it wasn't just like his dad was leaving. It was always more than that between them. His dad was his hero, his best friend, his first basketball coach, and still the one who had taught him the most. So much of what Wes already knew about the game, all the big stuff about teamwork and unselfishness and decision-making, he'd learned from his dad. Especially the part about making good decisions. Even at twelve, Wes knew that for a Navy SEAL, making good decisions could mean the difference between life and death.

Before he'd left to get on the plane that day, Wes said, "Weren't you supposed to be done after your last tour?"

His dad put his arms around him. Wes had grown a lot between fifth and sixth grade, but he still felt like a little boy when his dad's arms were around him.

"Turns out the job wasn't done," his dad said. "And you know what I always tell you about jobs."

"They don't finish themselves," Wes said.

Wes waited for his mom to say that the job was never going to be finished in Afghanistan. But she didn't. Wes had heard them go back and forth about Afghanistan, not arguing, just talking about it in the kitchen when they thought he was asleep upstairs, their voices getting loud sometimes. When Wes would get up in the morning, he'd say, "Were you and Dad fighting last night?" And she'd smile and tell him that they weren't fighting, just not giving in.

There was none of that the day they said good-bye, his mom not wanting this particular good-bye to be any harder than it needed to be.

"I'll be back before you know it," Michael Davies said to Wes, his strong arms still holding him tight. "And when I do come back, for good, I expect you to be twice the ballplayer you are now."

"I will be."

"Promise?"

"Promise."

Wes pulled away then, so he could look up at his dad, knowing there were tears in his eyes, but not caring.

"You just promise you'll come home."

"And I'll be twice the dad I am now," his dad had said.

But when his dad returned, he wasn't. Not even close.

THREE

NO ONE WAS QUITE SURE when the seventh-grade travel team in Annapolis had become the most glamorous one, at least before you started playing high school ball.

But it always had been, even before the formation of the Tri-State League and the chance to compete out of the region and all the way to the National Travel Basketball Association tournament, in South Carolina.

So there was that on the line for the Annapolis Hawks, along with the chance go on to play AAU ball, which was the first giant step toward getting a college scholarship someday.

Wes knew AAU ball got you seen. It got you noticed. High school ball could do that, too. But Wes was still two years away from being a freshman, and AAU ball was next season. It was another reason why this season was so important.

Just not the only reason.

It was more than that with Wes, even though he'd never talked about why with his friends, or even his mom. And he told his mom almost everything.

"You know," she said at the dinner, "I'm almost positive you said something on the way home from practice. But I must have missed it."

"I was kind of bummed, is all."

"Wow," she said, "I didn't pick up on that at all!"

He told her then about Dinero's pass hitting him in the face and feeling like a complete idiot in front of the team.

It was only the two of them, as usual. His dad no longer even came over for dinner. Wes still didn't understand why.

His mom slapped the table but was smiling at him as she did.

"Oh, the horror!" she said. "Well, that's it, we'll have to find you another sport. I forget, are you any good at skating? Of course, that would bring in the risk of getting hit in that adorable face by a puck."

"I'm glad you think this is funny," Wes said.

"You know I don't," she said. "And I would never make fun of you. But missing one pass doesn't sound to me like the end of the world."

"It wasn't just the pass!" Wes said. Now he was the one with the loud voice at the kitchen table. "It was that I wasn't paying attention."

"And, knowing you, it won't happen again," she said. "How did you play after that?"

"Okay, I guess."

"With you," his mom said, "that generally means a lot better than just okay."

They ate in silence for a few minutes. The quiet never seemed to bother either one of them. It was one more thing that he loved about her. She didn't know as much about basketball as his dad did. Wes was pretty sure that his dad knew more about basketball than anybody not coaching a team in high school or college or the pros. But his mom tried. She understood his dreams about making it to the nationals in travel ball, about AAU and college ball someday. And maybe even dreams that took him beyond college. She just didn't treat basketball like it was a matter of life and death.

When Wes looked up at her again, he said, "He's even better than I thought he was."

"Who?"

"Dinero."

She smiled again. "I kind of love that he calls himself that," she said.

"No kidding, Mom," Wes said. "When he makes a really good pass or play, he even rubs his fingers together the way that guy Johnny Football used to."

"And nobody thinks that's just a tad egotistical?"

"I think they would with anybody else," Wes said. "But somehow he even makes being egotistical look smooth."

"That's not you," she said.

"And never gonna be me."

"Do you get the feeling that the two of you are going to be a good team?" she said.

"We have to be," Wes said. "Or the Hawks will never be the team I think we can be."

"You know what your father always said," she said. "The beauty of basketball is five guys, one ball."

"Sometimes it's just two guys," Wes said, "having to figure it out. Curry and Durant did with the Warriors."

"And Davies and Rey will with the Annapolis Hawks," Christine Davies said.

There was another silence now, the longest yet, until Wes looked at her and said, "You think he might show up tonight?"

She slowly shook her head, the smile gone, almost as if it had never been there.

"Didn't he say he might?" Wes said.

"Your father says a lot of things these days, at least when he's around," she said. "He came home wounded this time, just not in the way that people think of a wounded soldier. And to make the pain go away, he drinks. I know you know that. It's another reason why we're apart right now."

"It's because he's hurting so bad."

"We all are."

"It's like we only see the damage," Wes said. "But dad has to live with it."

"I know," his mom said. "I know."

She asked if he would like some dessert; she'd bought his favorite: salted caramel ice cream. Wes said maybe later.

For now, they both knew where he was going.

Out to the basket his father had put up in the driveway, a driveway he'd expanded himself to give Wes more room to move around and work on his game. A driveway that had once been their place and now was just Wes's.

"I used to think it was some kind of joke when people would talk about kids who eat and sleep basketball," his mom said. "Not with you. You don't need ice cream. You're having basketball for dessert."

He managed a small smile now, even though it took some work. He was still feeling the sting of that pass.

FOUR

I T WASN'T THE SAME WITHOUT him.

None of it was.

It was still basketball. Wes could even appreciate the peace he felt, just him and the ball and the hoop, out here alone in the night, in a splash of light from the floodlight his dad had installed at the highest point of the garage.

Somehow the sounds were almost sweeter when he was out here. Sound of the ball on the dribble. Sound of the ball hitting the net. Even what the announcers called the "kiss" of the ball off the backboard when he'd bank one in.

The only sound that was missing was the sound of his dad's voice.

"You've got to finish, Wesley Davies. Finish the pass.
    Finish the drive. Finish the shot. Finish the job."
"You've got to get that shot off quicker, or somebody
        will be getting you."
"People always talk about what players can do in
        space. Well, guess who has to create that
        space? You do!"

But no matter how hard his dad worked him, no matter how much he was in Wes's ear, he still made it fun. He never acted like one of *those* dads. He wasn't Lonzo Ball's dad, the one who made you think you couldn't turn on ESPN without seeing him. Or hearing him. Wes never felt as if he were being pushed. His dad wasn't in his ear or in his head *that* way.

"We've always got to be clear on one thing," Michael Davies would say. "These are your dreams, not mine. And I'll never love those dreams as much as you will."

"But didn't you love basketball as much as I do when you were my age?" Wes asked him one time.

"I did," his dad had said. "But I didn't have the gift for it that you do."

"How did you know?"

"Because deep down you always know."

And he was always big on telling Wes that the great ones had to be selfish and unselfish at the same time, that finding the right balance was the trick.

"You got to know when to take it yourself," his dad liked to say. "But you got to know when to give it up."

Now Wes wondered whether he'd ever give up on his dad coming back to him, and to his mom, things going back to the way they were before he went away for the last time.

Wes wondered sometimes, especially when he was out here alone with basketball in the night, whether he'd ever get his dad back at all.

It was why his dreams had changed now. If he did have the gift for basketball that his dad told him he had, then he had to get more out of it than his dad ever had. Wes had to become the player his dad had always told him he could be. Was *convinced* Wes could be. His dad was the first to tell Wes, way before they moved here, how important AAU basketball was, how much it could do to get Wes to where he wanted to go. How it would be the next step for him once he got past seventh grade.

Wes worked on his first step now, off the right-hand dribble, off the left, back to his right, his dominant hand. But it wasn't only being quick off the dribble. You had to be able to put the brakes on, too, and change the direction. You had to create your space and get your shot.

Before somebody got you.

He didn't work on his passing tonight, didn't bring out the three passing nets his dad had bought for him, ones he could set up around the driveway, ones that could take a really hard pass and not topple over. When his dad was still here, still out here with him, Wes would complain when he'd miss a net with a pass and have to go chase down the ball.

"So don't miss," his dad would say, but always with a smile and a wink. His dad had never pushed him. If anything, he would slow Wes down when he thought he was trying too hard, or trying to do too much.

That's what had really happened at practice tonight: Even though Dinero was the one who'd thrown the pass, it was Wes who had missed. He knew he shouldn't be still fixed on it. But he was. When he'd think about it, he'd get mad at himself all over again, even as he told himself that Mom was right, that he'd never let anything like that happen again. He'd be ready next time. He *had* to be ready because he already knew he'd never played with a passer better than Dinero Rey.

Wes could pass, too. He was a forward who really could pass like a point guard. His best friend, Emmanuel Pike, always told him he was a little guy in a big guy's body, that someday Wes was going to be the most famous point forward in the world. As much as Wes's dad believed in him, Emmanuel seemed to believe in him just as much. And it made Wes work even harder, because he didn't want to make liars out of either one of them.

But Dinero?

He made the whole thing look easy. Like basketball came as easy to him as that smile. Like he was the seventh-grade version of Steph Curry. Now he and Dinero had been thrown together the way Steph and Kevin Durant had been thrown together. They'd sure made it work with the Warriors.

Two guys.

One ball.

It had been something going up against Dinero's team in sixth-grade ball, his team and Wes's making it to the finals of their league, Dinero's team winning by a basket in the end. Wes thought Dinero's team was more than a basket better than his, but Wes had pretty much played the game of his life in the finals—first triple-double of his life—and kept it close the whole way, before Dinero made a pass and got his team a layup at the very end.

That day he'd honestly felt it was big fun being Dinero's rival.

Now they were teammates.

So they weren't rivals anymore, right? He remembered the

weird grin Dinero had given him. It hadn't felt all that friendly.

Maybe they still *were* rivals.

Somehow Wes had to make sure they didn't get in each other's way. He couldn't let *anything* get in his way.

Or he'd never get his dad back.

FIVE

PRACTICE WAS EARLIER THAN USUAL on Thursday, five o'clock at the Boys and Girls Club.

Wes's school was the Wiley Bates Middle School, sixth through eighth. Rather than take the bus home and have only an hour or so before practice, he decided to spend the time a lot more productively, which meant with his guidance counselor, Joe Correa.

Other than the friends he'd made over the last year at Wiley Bates, Mr. Correa was pretty much the coolest guy in school and someone who felt more like a dad lately than his real dad. Wes knew that a lot of other seventh-graders, including Dinero, were tight with Mr. Correa, too. There was just something about him that made him relatable. It was a Mom word: *relatable*. She said it was a quality that the best teachers had, and you either had it or you didn't. Mr. Correa did.

He was about six three and had played high school ball when he was growing up in New York City. But he said he always knew he didn't have it in him to take the next step. Wes wasn't so sure about that. From time to time he'd seen Mr. Correa in some pickup games at the rec center, playing with some of his boys. As far as Wes could see, he still had some serious game, even as slow-footed as he was, and always seemed to be enjoying himself more than everybody on the court, as hard as you could see him trying to win.

"I always wanted basketball *in* my life," he told Wes after one of his pickup games. "But I knew it was never going to *be* my life."

"It's different with me," Wes said, "and always will be."

Mr. Correa grinned. "Always is a long time."

"I'm just sayin'," Wes said.

Now they were in his small office, one filled with books, not just on the shelves, but stacked on the floor. Mr. Correa taught English in all three grades at Wiley Bates and seemed to love reading and writing—and his books—the way Wes loved basketball.

"I didn't get a chance to ask you yesterday," Mr. Correa said. "How'd the first practice go?"

"Well, it started off terrible," Wes said, and told him about getting hit in the face.

Mr. Correa laughed.

"You too?" Wes said.

"What do you mean?"

"My mother thought it was funny, too," Wes said, "even though I came home thinking I had 'Wilson' imprinted across the side of my face."

Mr. Correa laughed again.

He was wearing his usual school outfit: khaki slacks; a pair of beat-up old-school Jordans; one of those shirts you could wear outside your pants. He had a young face and an easygoing smile.

If you didn't know he was a teacher, you probably could mistake him for a college kid.

"I did a lot better when we scrimmaged," Wes said.

"Shocker," Mr. Correa said.

"It's going to be serious ball on our team," Wes said.

"Shouldn't be any problem for a serious baller like you," Mr. Correa said. "You'll figure it out."

"It's gonna be a challenge," Wes said.

"New teams and new teammates usually are."

Wes said, "I almost felt like it was my first day of basketball school."

"Totally normal," Mr. Correa said.

Wes looked around, even though it was just the two of them. "If I tell you something, it stays in here, right?"

Mr. Correa said, "Like my books."

Wes blew out some air, making a big sound in the small office.

"Even after just one practice, I feel like it's Dinero's team."

"His world, and you're merely living in it?"

"Something like that," Wes said.

Mr. Correa ran a hand through his hair.

"That is his personality," he said, "and has been from the time he first walked through the doors of this school. He entered as a sixth-grader the way everybody else did. But he carried himself as if he'd been here his whole life."

"It's almost as if he'd already elected himself captain of the team," Wes said.

"My experience," Mr. Correa said, "is that really good point guards—and he's a really good point guard—always sort of feel that way. Maybe it's because they know they're going to have the ball the most."

"Every other team I've played on, the offense ran through me, even though I was playing forward."

"Because that's the way your dad taught you?" Mr. Correa said.

Wes nodded.

"From everything I've seen the last couple of years, he taught you really, really well. Have you talked about you and Dinero with him?"

"I haven't talked to him in a couple of weeks," Wes said. "He used to come for dinner at least once a week. But now he's not even doing that."

"Maybe he needs time," Mr. Correa said. "You can't lose faith."

"That's what my mom says."

"You've got two great parents, Wes. It's just that one of them is going through a very hard time."

"I feel like I've only got one parent right now," Wes said. "And maybe for always."

Mr. Correa smiled. "I thought we already went over this. Always is a long time."

The office was quiet then. It reminded Wes of his own house. Or maybe his life. It wasn't that way when his dad was still his dad. If he was in the house, boy, you *knew* he was in the house. When he was talking, about anything, with Wes or with his mom, it was as if he were in every room in the house at once.

That was before he'd gotten back from Afghanistan.

Before everything changed, and he would spend hour after

hour sitting in the small den where he and Wes used to watch games together, any kind of basketball game, college or pro. Sometimes, if it was a really big game, his mom would set up TV tables for them in there, and they'd watch from dinner all the way until it was time for Wes to go to bed. Unless there was another big game, and he got to stay up late.

Now it was all different. That room had become his dad's room. Sometimes he would have the television on, sometimes not. But he would be there alone, usually with a bottle of whiskey next to him and a glass.

Wes would wake up in the night and come downstairs if the television was still on, and his dad would still be in his chair, head back, snoring slightly, the bottle next to him empty most of the time.

It was as if he'd left the house even before he officially moved out and into the small apartment closer to the Naval Academy, on the other side of town.

"Was your dad drinking the last time you saw him?"

They had talked about that. They talked about everything. Sometimes Wes needed to talk about everything with someone other than his mother.

"He wasn't drinking the last time he came for dinner," Wes said, "because he was driving."

"It's a very good sign," Mr. Correa said, "that he's aware enough not to drink and drive."

"He was that night," Wes said.

"Did you two talk about basketball?"

"We hardly talked about anything," Wes said.

"And that was the last time you saw him."

"Not exactly."

"Not exactly?" Mr. Correa said. "What does that mean?"

"I didn't even tell my mom this," Wes said. "But you know the netting that separates the courts at the rec center? I couldn't see through it too well. But I thought I saw him up in the stands on the next court over. Sitting there by himself."

"Did you go over?"

"We were scrimmaging by then," he said. "And by the time we finished scrimmaging, whoever it was was gone."

He felt his throat tightening. It happened a lot when he thought about his dad.

"It was almost like I'd seen a ghost," Wes said, and then told Mr. Correa that maybe that figured, because his dad had pretty much become a ghost.

SIX

I T WAS DURING A WATER break at Boys and Girls that Emmanuel Pike said, "We are *definitely* not playing sixth-grade ball anymore."

"No," Wes said, "we are not."

"This is real," Emmanuel said.

"So real," Wes said.

Emmanuel was maybe two inches taller and fifteen pounds heavier than Wes, a power forward who could run the floor and defend and rebound and couldn't shoot to save his life. He was big and strong and played with heart and was the kind of solid role player every good team needed. His mother was a hairstylist, so Emmanuel had cool cornrows that were long, but not too long.

They were happy to get a break in the action because tonight it really had been serious ball with the Hawks, starting with Wes. He was making what his dad called good nerves work for him on this night, knowing he had to be impressing his coach, and his teammates. He was making his shots, making good decisions, using his length to defend, generally doing the one thing that his dad had always told him great players had to do:

He was imposing his will on the game.

He and Dinero were on the same side, but tonight they were sharing the ball, communicating with each other—even though this was only their second scrimmage as teammates—thinking along with each other. Neither one of them was showing off. It was as if they were too busy for that. More like they were showing each other the possibilities if they could play together across a whole season the way they were playing together tonight.

And Wes was seeing something else tonight:

That Dinero Rey wanted it as much as he did. It was something he couldn't hide, even behind that smile. He still wanted to be a coach on the floor—he couldn't help himself—sometimes he'd be moving other guys around even when it was Wes with the ball.

"Game's about filling open spaces," he said to Wes one time when Coach Bob Saunders had stopped play because he didn't like the way his biggest guys were boxing out.

"One of the first things my dad ever taught me," Wes said.

"He gonna come check us out one of these nights?" Dinero said.

"Soon," Wes said.

For some reason, he turned then and looked down to the double doors at the end of the court, almost like he could feel his dad's eyes on him. But no one was down there. He couldn't see anybody looking through the windows in the doors. Then Coach Saunders blew his whistle and they were back at it, Coach saying that he wanted to go even harder than they had all night for the last fifteen minutes.

"You never know which play is gonna be the one that might change everything," Coach said.

That was a thing with him, Wes could tell already. He said that some of the biggest basketball games he'd ever seen sometimes turned on the smallest moments. You just didn't know when those moments were coming. So you had to be ready.

Don't you worry, Wes wanted to say to his coach. Don't you worry about me.

I'll be ready.

The game ended up tied. Dinero and Wes's team ended up with the ball last. Coach had put in a few plays at each practice. But he told them he didn't want them to run a play now. He wanted them to get somebody open and score. He wanted them to make a play.

Wes was being guarded by Andy Rhule, another small forward on their team, one Wes could see was going to get a lot of playing time. Dinero was being guarded by another of the Hawks' point guards, Josh Amaro.

Coach had put twenty seconds on the clock, just to dial things up for everybody.

Dinero said nothing to Wes as he brought the ball up, just gave a little nod of his head to indicate that he wanted Wes on his right.

They had been killing it all night with high pick-and-rolls, and somehow, just with their eyes, Dinero and Wes decided they would run one more.

Twelve seconds.

Ten.

Dinero was dribbling the ball near the top of the key, Josh respecting how quick he was by giving him some room. As soon as Dinero took a step to his right, Wes flashed in and set himself at the foul line extended.

Dinero ran Josh into the screen.

Andy Rhule switched over to cover Dinero.

As soon as he did, Wes reverse-pivoted and cut down the left side of the lane. Open. In space. But then he saw two things, almost at the exact same moment:

Saw Dinero's pass headed straight for him.

But saw the kid who everybody knew was going to be their starting center, DeAndre Walker, moving over to cut Wes off.

Dinero saw DeAndre, too, and before his pass even reached Wes, he was flying down the *right* side of the lane, beating Andy Rhule, a clear path to the basket.

Instincts took over for Wes then. He didn't even catch the ball. Just reached out with his big hands and tapped it right back to Dinero, almost as if the ball had never touched his hands at all.

Dinero caught it in stride, laid the ball in off the backboard just as the horn sounded.

Wes always loved basketball.

Sometimes he just loved it a little more.

Dinero pointed at him. He pointed back. It was just one play, at the end of their second scrimmage. But maybe this deal was going to work out after all.

"Ball didn't even touch the ground once it left Dinero's hands," Coach Bob Saunders said. "Sometimes this game is just pure air."

And could make you feel as if you were walking on it.

Wes took one more look at the double doors at the far end. The feeling that his dad was there was stronger than ever. Maybe because he knew how much his dad would have loved that play.

But there was no one there.

SEVEN

COACH SURPRISED THEM AFTER WHAT was supposed to be their last practice of the week and said they were going to have one more, at eight o'clock Saturday morning at the rec center—he'd already booked the court time for them.

All he said in the email he blasted out was that he'd have a surprise waiting for them when they got there.

He did.

"We are going to have ourselves a no-holds-barred, no-coach scrimmage today," Coach Saunders announced.

He told them he wasn't going far, he'd be in another part of the rec center working on his own game for a change, so they wouldn't be completely unsupervised. Just a little bit, he said. He said that what he mostly wanted was for them to supervise themselves this morning, without him watching over them. Without them trying to impress him.

"I want you to impress yourselves today" is the way he put it.

They were the ones who were going to pick the teams. They were the ones who were going to keep the score and call the fouls, same as they would on the playground, where everybody always used the honor system. If they wanted to use set plays, they could. If they wanted to go all street, as he put it, and really make it a playground game, they could haul off and do that, too.

"Point is," Coach said, "I've seen how hard you've all been working, getting ready for the season. Today I just want you all to cut loose and play, and have fun. Get to know one another better that way. Don't be what you think I want you to be. Just be your own selves."

"So, you want us to be unplugged," Dinero said.

Coach grinned. "Not sure if you could be any more unplugged than you are already, son," he said. "All due respect."

"Better watch it, Coach," Emmanuel said. "You might affect the Money Man's confidence."

Coach shook his head, still grinning. "Couldn't do that if *I* tried," he said.

They all laughed, even Dinero.

Coach said he didn't want there to be any beefs or stare-downs or hurt feelings. The rule of the day was to cut loose. Not be afraid to show the best in their games, and maybe even the worst sometimes.

"I want this to be an hour of team bonding," he said.

"You want to know who wins?" Wes said.

"Nah," Coach said. "It'll be enough to know that you all know."

They tried to balance the teams out right. This was after the rest of the guys had decided that the way to have a fair game, and the best game, would be if Wes and Dinero were on different teams. Dinero got DeAndre as his big guy. Wes got Emmanuel.

From the start, it *was* the best game, everything Coach could have hoped for.

It was like one of those runs you'd get in the summer, on your favorite playground, even if you didn't know all of the other players in the game, everybody there just to show off *their* best game.

Casey Fisher, another of the Hawks' small forwards, was guarding Wes. Josh Amaro was guarding Dinero. And for the next hour, it seemed everybody on the court got a chance to shine.

But after a while, it became clear that the imaginary spotlight was shining brightest on only two of them:

Wes and Dinero.

They didn't keep calling their own number. They didn't dominate the ball, even though Dinero had it way more for his team than Wes did for his. But as much as Dinero did have it, as much showboating as he was doing every chance he got, it was still fun for Wes to watch, and even appreciate, even if you were on the other team. From all his time watching the NBA, Wes knew it was a little bit like watching Russell Westbrook, both before and after he stopped being teammates with Kevin Durant. No matter how much Westbrook loved to showboat—and Wes knew he did—and draw as much attention to himself, you still wanted to watch the way he could play the game, whether he was shooting or passing or getting another rebound on his way to another triple-double.

His game almost *demanded* that you watch him every time he had the ball in his hands, or was about to go get it off the boards, or had gotten an assist.

He even made you care.

It was a little like that with Dinero Rey, already.

But Wes kept up with him today. He held his own. He wasn't going to change who he was. But he wasn't going to let himself get shown up by Dinero, either.

Coach said to have fun?

Winning was fun.

Dinero kept breaking down the defense off the dribble, effortlessly. Sometimes he was happy to dish to DeAndre or Casey or Russ Adams, the Hawks' best shooting guard. Sometimes he'd make a playground move on a drive, or pull up and launch a three. Sometimes he'd chirp after he made a play or a basket.

Sometimes he'd rub his fingers together in his Money Man gesture.

They would probably always be totally different on the court, but Wes knew he loved watching Dinero play.

And was going to love beating him even more.

They only had the court for a couple of minutes more. Dinero broke past Josh one more time, did a little stutter-step as if he were pulling up in the lane. E ran at him from underneath the basket. Dinero, smiling, drove past him and laid the ball in.

Game tied.

It was decided, because they could all see they were up against the clock, that if Wes's team scored, they won. If not, they'd play until next basket won.

"I'll take Wes," Dinero said.

"Fine with me," Casey Fisher said.

Bring it, Wes said to himself.

Wes gave a quick look at Emmanuel and winked. It was Wes's way of telling his friend to be ready.

Wes knew he was ready, because he knew exactly what he wanted to do. Had it worked out inside his head. He remembered a time when his dad had shown him the end of what he said was one of his favorite NBA games ever played. Bulls against the Knicks, Madison Square Garden. It was when Michael Jordan was only a couple of weeks back after having gone off to play minor-league baseball in the middle of his career.

By the time the game was down to the last fifteen seconds, Jordan had already scored fifty-five points.

"Wasn't even close to being in basketball shape yet," Michael Davies had said. "And he goes in there and drops a double-nickel on them."

He paused the video and then said, "Watch what happened then."

Bulls had the last shot. Everybody in the Garden knew who was taking it.

Only Jordan didn't shoot.

He looked like he was going to shoot, but then at the last second he passed to the Bulls' center, who dunked the ball, and the Bulls won by that basket.

Dinero covered Wes closely all the way up the court. A couple of times, he flicked out those fast hands of his and tried to steal the ball. One time, Wes spun away from him. Another, he just angled his body so it was between him and Dinero.

When he got to the top of the key, Dinero still all over him,

Wes went behind his back, something he'd never do in a real game, and broke into the clear at the free-throw line.

DeAndre had no choice but to come up on him.

By the time he did, Wes was already rising up into his jump shot.

DeAndre even yelled, trying to distract him.

Yell your head off, Wes thought, right before he fired a bullet pass to Emmanuel underneath the basket.

E laid the ball in.

Game time.

Dinero got to Wes first. And there was that weird grin again, the one that made Wes feel like it was anything but a smile.

"You got me today," Dinero said. "I'll get you next time."

"Next time," Wes said, "it'll be a real game. And we'll be on the same team."

Dinero was still grinning.

"Yeah," he said. "Won't we, though."

EIGHT

IS MOM, WES KNEW, ALWAYS loved horses, from the time she first rode as a little girl. She had been a champion rider all the way through high school, but had finally given up competing when she went to the University of Maryland. But she still loved being around them. So, a couple of days a week, when she was done with her job as librarian at Annapolis High School, she volunteered at a barn outside of town where developmentally challenged people, children and adults, got up on horses and would slowly be walked around a ring.

"It's as much therapy for me as it is for them," she told Wes. "It's not just good for their spirit, it's good for my soul."

Another time she said, "Being at the barn reminds me that it doesn't have to be challenging to be happy."

Wes wasn't sure if she was talking about the people she helped or the horses or herself.

Two days a week, then, he'd come home to an empty house after school. It didn't bother Wes. He already felt lonely enough a lot of the time, without his dad in his life. He just kept trying to use his alone time to keep himself focused on getting better at basketball, because basketball was the one thing in his life he felt he could control.

If things did work out the way he hoped they would, there was no way his dad wouldn't want to be a part of this basketball season. This was Wes's first chance to show off his skills on an elite team like the Hawks. It was all part of the plan. Of course Wes wanted him and Dinero to be a good team, to figure it out the way Steph and Durant had. Of course he wanted the Hawks to be a great team.

But the real team was supposed to be him and his dad.

The next practice for the Hawks was scheduled for Saturday morning at the Annapolis Rec Center. The Saturday after that, the regular season started. When Wes got home from school on Friday afternoon, a barn afternoon for his mom, he didn't even take time to make himself a snack. He changed into his old Under Armour sneakers—he didn't wear the new ones outside on the driveway—and his cool blue Wizards shorts and the long-sleeved shooting shirt all the members of the Hawks had been given, got his basketball, and went right outside and got to work.

He started today with a drill he used to do with his dad all the time: Bounce the ball high to his left or right, run and catch it before it hit the ground, and shoot.

Run to the spot, catch, shoot.

Again and again.

As usual, he could hear his dad's voice inside his head:

No wasted motion. Up and into the shot.

"C'mon," Wes heard. "You're taking too much time to release it."

He stopped.

The voice wasn't inside his head now. It was coming from the end of the driveway.

NINE

THE BEARD HE'D COME HOME with from Afghanistan had gotten longer, and he'd stopped trimming it, Wes saw. He was wearing the old white-and-orange Orioles cap he'd owned for as long as Wes could remember. Faded blue jeans that were too big on him and a black T-shirt.

As he made his way up the driveway, he was still limping. He'd never really explained to Wes or his mom why.

Wes wanted to toss the ball and run and hug him. But something kept him from doing that. Maybe the fear that he wouldn't be hugged back. Or maybe his dad looked so weak that Wes actually was afraid he might knock him over.

So he stayed where he was, right in front of the basket, ball cocked on his hip.

But he could feel himself smiling. Realizing in that moment how little it took for *him* to be happy.

He didn't know why his dad was here. Just that he was here.

"You're running after the ball like you've still got your backpack on," his dad said. "You know that in a game you're not gonna be covered by guys as old and slow as me, right?"

"Maybe slow," Wes said. "But not old."

"Old as the navy," his dad said.

"Mom's not here," Wes said, without being asked.

"I know."

"Is that why you picked now to come?" Wes said.

"It's not that I don't want to see your mom," he said. "But today I wanted to see you."

"I'm here every day and every night," Wes said.

Just like that, he knew his smile was gone.

"Know that, too," his dad said.

Neither one of them said anything until his dad said, "I felt like you were a little slow with your release the other night at practice."

"I *knew* you were there," Wes said. "I just knew it."

His dad lifted his shoulders and dropped them, as if even that took a lot of effort. Tipped the Orioles cap back on his head. "Old habits," he said, "die hard."

"You could have come closer to the court," Wes said. "A lot of parents do—Coach doesn't mind. And I could have introduced you to Coach and the guys."

"I was fine where I was," he said. "Watching from a distance."

Wes thought, And not only with my basketball.

"Where's your car?" Wes said. "I didn't hear it."

"Parked a few blocks away," he said. "Do a little extra walking every chance I get. Trying to build the strength up in the leg."

Again: He never said what happened to make him limp or why he lost strength in his leg. His mom had tried to get it out of him when he was first back and still living in the house. He'd say he wasn't ready to talk about it. Never specifying what *it* was, whether he was talking about the war or what had happened there or his injured leg. Or all of it.

Her questions only made him quieter, if that was even possible. It was like he was watching them from a distance even when he was still in the house. And they were watching him the same way.

"It's good to see you, Dad," Wes said now.

"Good to see you, big boy."

"How are you doing really?"

"Doing okay," he said. Then added, "Really."

Wes was about to tell him that he didn't seem okay, that he seemed the total, complete opposite of okay, almost like he'd turned into a total, complete new person. But what was the point? If he knew that, so did his dad.

They stood there, awkwardly staring at each other. Wes could still feel the connection between them, even here. But sometimes it was as if he were still as far away as Afghanistan. Wes would tell his mom sometimes that she could find out all the details if she wanted.

"I'll find out when your father tells me," she said. "Or tells us."

"He needs us to help him," Wes said.

Then she said, "Not until he's ready for it. And right now he can't even help himself."

But today, he was here to help Wes, as it turned out.

"You can't keep letting that other boy run the whole show," his dad said. "Like they used to say: Not enough mustard in the whole world to cover that kid."

They both knew who he meant.

"I'm not, Dad," Wes said. "I'm trying to figure out how we can run it together. And you're the one who's always told me you can't be the best player you can be without being the best teammate you can be."

"Wish I could take credit for that one," his dad said. "That one came from my old high school coach."

He motioned with his hands for Wes to pass him the ball. Wes snapped off a hard chest pass that wasn't too hard, extending his arms and his hands, turning his wrists out as he released the ball.

Michael Davies caught the ball and then rolled it around in his hands.

"That other boy?" he said.

"His name is Dinero."

His father laughed. "That his real name?"

"Nickname. Danilo is his real first name. Like Danilo Gallinari, the guy from the NBA."

"Well, whether it's Danilo or Dinero, you make sure that boy shows you the proper respect," he said. "He's a good enough player that he has to know how good *you* are. Probably the best he's ever played with. But he acts like he's the boss out there on the court. He can't go more than a few minutes without doing something to draw attention to himself. Like he thinks there needs to be a spotlight on him all the time."

"I'm not feeling that, Dad, I'm really not. He just has more street ball in his game."

"Well, I'm *seeing* that. Saw it in that scrimmage, for sure."

How much of their practices had he been watching?

"How much have you seen?"

"Enough to know that I know what I'm talking about."

He snapped off a hard bounce pass back at Wes. Wes grinned and fired one back at him.

"We'll get it figured out," Wes said.

"You sure?" his dad said.

"Yeah."

"He thinks it has to be on his terms. You can tell he's been spoiled into thinking that, probably every step of the way."

Wes started to say something. His dad held up a hand.

"Remember something," his dad continued. "He might think he's better than you. But he's not."

"Truth? Best I've played with yet."

"I've told you your whole life," his dad said, "best means more than most talented."

At least, Wes thought, he's trying to be my dad, whether I agree with everything he's saying or not.

"Listen," his dad said, "I gotta get going."

"Why don't you hang around until Mom gets home?" Wes said. "Stay for supper."

"Maybe one day next week," he said.

He smiled now, even with his eyes, like he really meant it.

"You know what my favorite song is, right?"

Wes did. He couldn't remember the name of the old singer, just the name of the song.

"'I Won't Back Down,'" he said.

"The guy who wrote it died," his dad said. "People, they die in this world."

Then *his* smile was gone. "Anyway, I got to be going."

Michael Davies turned and walked down the driveway, made a left when he got to the sidewalk, and then was gone.

Wes wanted to run after him, the way he'd wanted to run and hug him. But he didn't do that, either. Instead, he stood there with the ball in his hands until he said, "Love you."

He was the only one who heard.

TEN

I T WAS FIVE MINUTES BEFORE the first game of the
season. The gym at the rec center—a home game against the
Prince George's County Pistons—and the bleachers across
from the two home benches were already full.

Wes had just taken his last shot of warmups, a free throw,
never leaving the court until he made it, always telling himself it
was the point his team needed to win the game. Now he was at
the Hawks' bench, taking off his shooting shirt. He always wore
number thirteen. It was the number his dad had worn at Navy
because it had been Steve Nash's number with the Mavericks
and the Suns. His dad, Wes knew, had always been a Nash guy.
He said that nobody ever thought Nash would ever get close
to being a big-time star in the NBA, because of his size. But
he went on to be named MVP, not just once—twice—mostly
because, Wes's dad said, he played the same kind of beautiful
and unselfish floor game that made everyone he played with
look better.

"Other players were faster and bigger and stronger and
could jump higher than Steve Nash," his dad said. "Nobody was

tougher or tougher-minded. Or more creative when it came to making the other guys around him better."

Now Wes stared across the court at the bleachers, trying to spot his dad. But he could not.

Emmanuel saw where Wes was looking.

"Don't see him?" Emmanuel said.

"Nah."

"He still might show up."

"Like he showed up at the house without telling me he was coming," Wes said.

Wes kept staring, his eyes moving from side to side through the crowd, up and down the bleachers. He saw his mom, sitting in the second row with Emmanuel's mom and dad. She saw that he saw her, and smiled and waved. Wes gave her a small wave back.

"I hear the Pistons are loaded with scorers," Emmanuel said.

"E?" Wes said. "Everybody in this league is loaded."

Emmanuel turned and put out his fist so Wes could pound it with his own.

"Would we want it any other way?" he said.

"*No* way," Wes said.

Dinero came walking over, big smile on him, of course.

"You guys follow my lead today," he said, "all the way to a W."

Wes smiled back at him.

"Best thing about the Hawks is that we have a team of leaders," he said. "And every one of our guys is ready to put it on their guys."

Dinero held his gaze for a second, like they were having a contest to see who would stop smiling first, then turned to Emmanuel.

"Number Thirteen sounds ready to me," he said.

Emmanuel said, "You have no idea."

"Let's hope so," Dinero said to Wes.

Wes didn't recognize any of the players on the Prince George's team, not even from summer ball. But the guys on the starting fives introduced themselves to one another before the coin flip to determine which team would get the ball first. The kid who Wes would be guarding introduced himself as Matt Riley. He was about the same height as Wes, red haired, freckles covering his face.

Wes grinned when they shook hands and said, "You think there are two whiter kids in the whole state of Maryland than the two of us?"

"How about the whole world?" Matt said.

"Have a good one," Wes said.

"You too."

"Just not *too* good," Matt said.

The ref flipped a silver dollar. Wes called heads. It was. They'd get the ball first. When he and the rest of the starters were back in the huddle, Coach Saunders said, "Play the next play as the one that might make all the difference. You'll win as a team, so trust your teammates. If you want to do it all yourself, go play on one of the side courts."

They put their hands together in the middle of the circle and went out to play the season, which felt like the biggest of Wes's life. His eyes quickly searched the bleachers one last time before the ref handed him the ball so he could inbound it to Dinero.

If his dad was over there somewhere, he had managed to hide in plain sight.

By now he was as good at that as he'd once been at basketball.

ELEVEN

THE ELITE TEAM IN THE first half, in their first game in their elite league, wasn't the Hawks. And the best player in the game wasn't Wes. Or Dinero.

It was the Pistons' point guard, the one guarding Dinero and the one he was supposed to be guarding at the other end.

His name was Tate Brooks. He was a couple of inches taller than Dinero, and just as fast. Everything about him, even his looks, reminded Wes of Chris Paul. He even wore number 3, the same as Paul did.

Tate Brooks wasn't as slick with the ball as Dinero was. He couldn't make the flashy-looking passes that Dinero could. But he didn't try. It was as if he tried to make every play and every shot as clean as it could possibly be. And was dominating Dinero at both ends, and dominating the game.

No smiles from him. No change of expression, even when he would make a shot or a pass. No look-at-me to him. When he'd get a basket or an assist, his response was to get right back on defense. Or get up on Dinero and pressure him all the way up the court. Wes couldn't help but think how much fun it would be to play with a point guard like that.

And the better he played, the more frustrated Dinero got, the more he tried to do too much, as if Tate Brooks simply didn't understand that it was Dinero who was supposed to be the star of Hawks versus Pistons. Dinero who was supposed to be the point guard to watch.

On the last Pistons' possession of the first quarter, Tate easily beat Dinero off the dribble again. Dinero fouled him hard as he went by, making no attempt to make a play on the ball, and the ref whistled him for a flagrant foul. Wes didn't think that Dinero was doing anything dirty. He was frustrated, more angry at himself than anything else. Tate didn't get angry, just went to the free-throw line and knocked down both shots. The Pistons kept the ball. Tate fed their big man for a layup. The Pistons were ahead, 20–8.

When the Hawks got back to their bench, Coach Saunders pulled Dinero aside, spoke quietly to him, then turned and told Josh Amaro to report in. Josh would start the second quarter at point, not Dinero.

Wes watched to see how Dinero took it. He took it well, making a point—or a show—of patting Josh on the back and telling him to get out there and kill it. "Get me the lead," he said to his teammates. Somehow he had a way of making himself the show even when he was being asked to take a seat for a few minutes.

Josh was the same in the game as he was at practice: He didn't try to be someone he wasn't, starting with Dinero. But he had talent and brains, and had to know that he would be starting on most teams in the Tri-Valley League. On the rare occasions when they'd be on the same side in scrimmage, Wes loved playing with Josh. He ran the plays the way they were drawn up, seemed to have a good grasp of Coach's motion offense, and genuinely wanted the other four guys on the court with him to do well.

As the Hawks began to climb back into the game over the first few minutes of the second quarter, it was Wes who was doing well, mostly because Josh kept getting him the ball first chance he got.

On the Hawks' first three possessions of the quarter, Wes hit a jumper from the right wing, then one from the left wing, before he and Josh ran a high pick-and-roll and Josh fed him for a layup.

They'd cut the Pistons' lead in half. Next time down, Josh gave the ball to Wes on the left side, Wes beat Matt Riley, looked like he might go all the way to the basket before he made a sweet no-look to Emmanuel. And for the first time in the game, Wes was aware of some real noise coming from the Hawks' fans in the bleachers. The Hawks finally tied the game when Wes took an outlet pass from Emmanuel, saw Josh take off down the right sideline, and threw an over-the-head, two-hand pass about fifty feet that caught Josh right in stride, and well ahead of the defense.

The Pistons' coach called for time.

Day late and a dollar short, Wes thought to himself, his dad's voice inside his head again as he remembered all the times when he'd be watching a game on TV with his dad, college or pro, and one of the teams would go off on a rip before the other team's coach would stand up and call time. And his dad would say, "He should have called that timeout two possessions ago."

The two teams played even the rest of the second quarter. Coach finally put Dinero back in for Josh, even though the

Hawks had been playing better without him. Dinero made the most of those last three minutes of the half, though, and the matchup between Dinero and Tate finally looked like a fair fight. Just before the horn sounded, Dinero made the play of the game thus far by timing Tate's dribble perfectly as Tate tried to drive past. Seemingly in one perfect move he stole the ball and fed Emmanuel with a pass that hit him perfectly in stride for an easy two right before the horn.

Wes thought that Dinero was still pounding the ball too much, still seemed too caught up more in winning the matchup with Tate than winning the game for the Hawks. But at least over those last three minutes of the half, he looked more like himself and the player he was supposed to be.

Even if today the only one who seemed to be following his lead was himself.

"Even though they came back a little the last part of the quarter," Coach Saunders said, "we've still got momentum on our side. But remember something: Momentum can be a funny old dog sometimes. And if you're not careful, he'll run away from you."

Coach, they all knew, had a lot of dog references.

Emmanuel grinned and raised a hand. "Does that mean you'd like us to keep the pressure on and keep playing like we're behind?"

"E," Coach said, "how lucky am I that I've got you to translate for me?"

They did keep the pressure on in the third quarter. The Hawks were starting to run now, and that was when Dinero was at his best. The whole team could feel him feeling it now.

But the one who was really feeling it, now that a really good game had broken out, was Wes Davies.

He got hot again, same as he did at the start of the second quarter when Josh was feeding him the ball. Now Dinero was, too. Fact was, he should have been doing it even more than he was. But he was still fixed on showing up Tate.

Even in the flow of the game the way he was, even picking up his own game again, Wes wondered whether everybody else could see what was happening: Dinero looking away from Wes sometimes when Wes was open and trying to break down Tate off the dribble. Still pounding it too much. But even if nobody else noticed, Wes did. He knew. He always knew the way things were supposed to be going, how the game was supposed to *flow*. How it was supposed to *look*.

Now he also knew that things continued to look up for the Hawks, no doubt, after that terrible beginning to the game. They were doing much better. Way better. But they could have been doing even better than that. Wes could see that Dinero wanted their first win as much as he did.

Even if it had to be on his terms.

His ball.

The Hawks were ahead by a basket at the end of the third quarter. Then the Pistons were ahead by two, four minutes into the fourth. There was a three-on-two break for the Hawks, almost like the drill they'd been doing the night Wes caught that pass in the face, when Dinero held on to the ball too long again, got himself jammed up in the middle before he made the pass he should have made to Wes, who'd gotten two long strides clear of

Matt Riley. Dinero ended up forcing a pass to Emmanuel, too hard and too far away from the basket, and the ball went off E's hands and out of bounds.

As the ref went to collect the ball, Wes went over to Dinero, couldn't help himself and said, "I was open."

Dinero stared at him, then shrugged, said, "My bad," and walked away. Wes couldn't tell whether he meant it or not. Didn't matter, though. The game was still tied, 42–42, thirty seconds left, Hawks' ball, in front of their own bench. Wes and Dinero were there. Coach told them to run a weak-side pick play.

"Then one of you figure out something doggoned wonderful," he said.

They both nodded. Emmanuel was standing underneath their basket, watching them. Wes nodded at him, briefly touched a hand to the top of his head. It meant for him to flash up, first chance he got, and set a screen on Matt.

Wes inbounded the ball to Dinero. Dinero checked the game clock, slowly dribbled toward the top of the key, then kept going to his left. As soon as he did that, Emmanuel Pike came hard from the right side of the lane and set a perfect pick on Matt Riley.

Wes had his choice: Cut inside and down the lane to the basket, or break to the outside. But there was too much traffic clogging the lane. Wes ran for the right corner, wide-open, nobody on him. Matt and the Pistons' center had both stayed with Emmanuel.

As Wes ran, he watched Dinero the whole time, making sure he was ready for the pass he knew was coming.

Dinero was still dribbling.

He crossed over now, Tate right on him, got himself into the lane, where there was still a ton of traffic. Wes checked the game clock, ran for the basket. Twenty seconds now. Still time for Dinero to give it up.

He wasn't giving it up.

With ten seconds left he pushed up an off-balance teardrop, somehow getting it underneath Tate's arm, almost flinging it in the direction of the basket.

They all watched then as the ball, with hardly any spin on it, bounced high off the backboard, came down on the front of the rim, hung there for what felt like a minute and not the last second of regulation.

And then fell through the basket.

Hawks by two.

Pistons out of timeouts. Their shooting guard inbounded the ball to Matt Riley, closest Piston to him. But Wes knew Matt only had one plan: Get the ball to Tate Brooks, who'd shaken free of Dinero.

Wes backed off Matt, watching his eyes the whole time, got himself into the passing lane between Matt and Tate, intercepted Matt's pass as if it had been intended for him.

He could have walked in and made a meaningless, show-off basket before the final horn. Instead, he dribbled toward the basket, veered off at the last second, ended up back in the corner.

Ball game.

TWELVE

WES AND EMMANUEL WERE AT the Annapolis Ice Cream Factory on Main Street. Wes's mom had dropped them there after the game.

Emmanuel was eating his favorite at the Ice Cream Factory, strawberry in a big bowl, with colored sprinkles on top. Wes thought everything about it was wrong. He had gone old-school: banana split, two scoops, vanilla and chocolate, chocolate sauce, whipped cream.

"Got a question," Emmanuel said.

"Shoot."

Emmanuel made a snorting sound. "Shouldn't we leave that to Dinero?"

"Not. Funny."

But they both knew it was.

"My question is this: How come you needed comfort food when we won the game?"

"You know I need about as much of an excuse to eat ice cream as you do," Wes said. "And I never need an excuse to eat ice cream."

"Except after the game you said we needed ice cream now," E said. "And you stepped on *now* pretty hard."

"So *now* we're eating ice cream," Wes said. "And I don't need comforting. I need you to admit that we both saw something on that last play we didn't like."

"We did," E said. "Hundred percent."

They talked it through then. Agreed that there was no way that Dinero didn't see how open Wes was. Dinero saw everything on the court the same way Wes did. They also agreed there was no way that Dinero had suddenly forgotten how hot Wes had been the whole game. Or that he thought he was making the right play because he thought he could get a better shot.

What he got, they both *really* agreed, was a bad shot that happened to go in.

"It's supposed to be about all of us," Wes said. "And what I keep thinking that Dinero wants it to be about us right after it's about him. You hear what I'm saying?"

Emmanuel said, "Loud and clear."

Wes said, "He didn't like the way he got shown up by that guy Tate early. So he was fixed on making up for it with a hero play at the end. Even if it had cost us."

"He's lucky it *didn't* cost us," Emmanuel said.

"Right is right, like my dad says. He also says if you're right, you don't run."

"So," E said, "what are we gonna do about this?"

Wes spooned more ice cream into his mouth. It didn't make him feel any better. But being with Emmanuel always did. Going through what he was going through with his dad, trying to get through it and still keep his focus on basketball, was always made a little easier because he had E as his wing man. Wes would never compare what he was going through to being a Navy SEAL, not in a million years. But sometimes he pretended like he and Emmanuel Pike were in the same unit. Tight like that.

Wes checked his phone. It was almost time for his mom to pick them up.

"You think I should talk to him?" Wes asked.

"I don't know if he's gonna change," E said. "I know he can see what a good player you are. But he also sees some kind of threat."

"I gotta convince him that he's wrong," Wes said. "I don't know how. But I do have one idea worth trying."

Wes met Dinero at the rec center at eleven o'clock on Sunday morning. Wes's mom drove him. Dinero's dad drove him. Wes was waiting out front when Dinero and his dad pulled up. He watched as Dinero's dad got out of the driver's side and came around and hugged Dinero before getting back behind the wheel.

Before the car, a black Jeep, pulled away, Dinero's dad rolled down the window on the passenger's side, and Wes heard him say, "Love you, star. Go shine like you can."

"Love you, too, Papa," Dinero said.

Wes and Dinero had each brought their own basketball. Maybe, Wes thought, that figured.

I've got one ball; he's got another.

"Glad you called," Dinero said, giving Wes a quick high five. "I was just gonna veg and watch football today. Maybe shoot around a little in the backyard at halftime."

Wes knew from the other guys on the team that Dinero's dad, a lawyer in Annapolis, had built him a full court in their backyard, with a free-throw line, a three-point line, a lane, everything. They said that during the summer there were pickup games on Saturday mornings, mostly with seventh- and eighth-graders.

"I just thought that we could work on some stuff together," Wes said. "Maybe get to know each other's games better."

Dinero smiled, but it didn't feel to Wes like one of his happy smiles. "Fine with me, Thirteen."

It had always been Wes's theory that he did his best thinking on a court, with a ball in his hands. Maybe, he figured, if it was only him and Dinero on the court, they could talk in Wes's real first language:

Basketball.

Wes decided it was worth a try. They could only make this work if they worked together. Maybe they could be more than teammates. They could be friends.

That was the plan, anyway.

They had fun.

There was a game going on at the next court, five on five, a bunch of guys in it that Wes recognized from Mr. Correa's usual game. But he wasn't out there this morning. The court on the other side of the grown-ups' game was empty at eleven o'clock. So, for now, Wes and Dinero didn't have to worry about people showing up and wanting to use the court they were on.

They started out playing a game of H-O-R-S-E, Dinero finally winning on a three-pointer from the right corner that Wes missed twice. Wes had to hand it to the guy. Dinero didn't have much weakness to his game.

Then they played a game of one-on-one, to seven baskets. Dinero finally won that one, too, with a drive to his left—his left-handed dribble as sure and strong as his right—faking Wes into the air before he banked home the winner.

It made Dinero happy.

Very happy, with a smile as genuine as any Wes had seen on Dinero.

They had joked and chirped on each other the whole game. But they both knew it was serious ball, especially at the end.

Yet it didn't bother Wes so much to lose a contest like this, one that came down to the final shot. He'd shown his own skills along the way, proven that he could keep up with Dinero step for step.

They sat down on the floor and drank from the water bottles they'd both brought.

"Do your parents always tell you to hydrate?" Wes said.

"In two languages," Dinero said.

"You think LeBron hydrates?" Wes said.

Dinero laughed. "Only if he feels like it," he said. "When you're as great as he is, you make your own rules."

"But he's an awesome teammate," Wes said. "That's what everybody says."

"Doesn't mean he doesn't make the rules," Dinero said. "The king does what he wants."

Wes nodded.

"Is LeBron your favorite player?"

Dinero shook his head. "Steph," he said. "I like that he stayed the man in Golden State even after Durant got there."

"But wasn't Durant MVP of the finals?"

"Game still runs through Steph," Dinero said. "Always will." The grin now, the one that wasn't quite a smile.

Wes thought, Are we talking about them, or are we talking about us?

He changed the subject. "You like working on stuff by yourself?" he said. "I do."

"I guess," Dinero said. "But after a while I get bored."

Wes never did.

"I already know what I can do," Dinero said. "I'd always rather play a game."

"Games help me get better," Wes said. "But sometimes I want to be alone and just work."

"You work," he said to Wes, grin back in place. "I play."

"Is there a difference?" Wes asked him, honestly wanting to know, because he didn't think so.

"I don't know, I don't think about it all that much," Dinero said. "Maybe it's because basketball was never hard for me."

He didn't make it sound as if he were bragging. Just stating a fact. Like he was telling Wes his cell phone number.

"You do make it look pretty easy," Wes said.

Just because he did.

"I just look at it, like, basketball is something I was meant to do," Dinero said. "Like it was my ticket to where I wanted to go."

"College ball?" Wes said.

"Steph didn't stop after Davidson," Dinero said. "Why should I?"

He made it sound as if they were the same, him and Steph, even though he was only in the seventh grade. Wes put it to him this way: "You sound so sure."

"Sure as you and me are sitting here," Dinero Rey said.

He took another swig of water. "You want to get after it one more time?"

"Okay," Wes said. "But I better warn you: No way you're taking me twice in the same day."

"Well then," Dinero said, "since it's Sunday morning, you better say a prayer, dude."

"I know you're just coming with more chirp," Wes said.

They both stood.

They'd used Dinero's ball in the first game. Wes picked it up. "Shoot for it?" he said.

"You take it," Dinero said. "Even if you get the lead, it won't last long."

"You sound like Mr. Correa going on about Shakespeare," Wes said. "All I hear is blah-blah-blah."

Wes had never loved playing one-on-one. Even though so much of basketball was you against somebody else, straight up, Wes had always looked at it as a game within a much bigger game. Wes Davies knew that people around the world called soccer "the beautiful game." But as far as he was concerned, they had it wrong. Basketball was the beautiful game, a game of motion, of passing and shooting, guarding and being guarded. One-on-one wasn't real ball, not to Wes. Real ball was ten guys out there, and ten times the possibilities.

That was real ball.

The only thing real for him right now was that he didn't plan on losing to Dinero again this morning.

Wes went up early, 4–2. But Dinero got hot in the middle of the game, even making a crazy fallaway with Wes all over him, to pull within one, 6–5. His ball. Winners out. They checked the ball out on top. Dinero crossed over on Wes, got a step on him, drove right, tried to rush a runner before Wes could use his long arms on him. Wes was ready and blocked it cleanly.

Dinero called a foul.

Wes knew it wasn't. He knew it was a clean block. But they were using the honor system, even if Wes didn't think Dinero was showing much honor right now. He didn't say anything or change expression. He just went and retrieved the ball, keeping himself calm, and handed it back to Dinero.

"Check," he said.

This time Dinero went left. Put on a burst off the dribble, stopped as quickly as he'd started, tried to fake Wes into the air the way he had at the end of the last game.

Fool me once, Wes thought.

He didn't bite. And proceeded to block *another* shot, as cleanly as before. Dinero didn't say a word. He had to know he couldn't call two fouls in a row, not this close to game time. He raced back to the outside. Dinero came out, but got too close to him. Wes stutter-stepped, blew past him, laid the ball in. It was 6–all. Now it was *game time*.

Wes went to the top of the key. Dinero checked him. There was only the sound of their breathing between them. Sound of the air.

And before Wes put the ball on the floor, he knew how he was going to win the game. Just like that. It almost made him smile. He prided himself on thinking one move ahead. Now this move had come to him.

Dinero wasn't as close as he'd gotten the play before, not wanting Wes to drive past him again and end the game with another layup. He watched as Wes calmly raised the ball over his head.

And then Wes was bringing the ball down, bouncing it hard between them, but at an angle, so it went flying in the direction of the right corner.

Dinero was slow to react. Wes ran underneath the ball like an outfielder running and getting himself underneath a long fly ball. He caught it before Dinero could catch up with him. Then he squared himself like he was alone in his driveway and put up a long jumper that hit nothing but net.

"Hey!" Dinero yelled, his voice sounding. "Hey, you can't do that, pass the ball to yourself!"

"Wasn't a pass," Wes said. "Just a real long dribble. It's called leading the ball. Look it up."

"That should be a travel," Dinero said. "Or a double dribble. It should be something."

"Here's what it is," Wes said. "Seven–six, me."

The next thing he said came out of him before he could stop it. Or maybe there was a part of him that didn't want to stop it.

"I just threw myself the pass you should have thrown me yesterday," he said.

Dinero had been walking to retrieve the ball. He stopped now.

Slowly turned around. Just like that, it was as if a dark cloud had passed in front of his face.

"You're not gonna let it go, are you?" he said.

"I was joking," Wes said.

"It didn't sound like joking to me," Dinero said. "You tell me you were open yesterday, and now today you bring it up again. You got a problem with me?"

Everything was suddenly more serious than the game.

"No," Wes said. "You got a problem with me making a little joke?"

"My *problem*," Dinero said, "is that you still have a problem with a game we won. On a shot that I made at the buzzer."

Wes thought about reminding him that it was a lucky shot, but knew that would only make things worse. He hadn't come here today looking to start a fight, just a basketball friendship.

"You told me the first night of practice," Wes said, "to be ready if I was open. Well, yesterday I was *wide* open."

They stood staring at each other. Dinero hadn't moved. Neither had Wes. Neither one of them giving any ground.

"You're not always my first option," Dinero said. "Maybe you need to get that in your head."

"But I should have been," Wes said. "Everybody knew that."

"Well, everybody didn't have the rock," Dinero said. "I did."

Then he flashed a strained smile and, without saying another word, without saying good-bye, walked over and picked up his ball, and grabbed the little gym bag in which he'd carried his water bottle, and walked out of the gym.

Taking his ball and going home.

THIRTEEN

JUST LIKE THAT, THINGS CHANGED between them, as if Dinero had smacked him with the ball all over again.

His ball.

If you watched the next two practices for the Hawks, you might not have noticed things were different between Dinero and Wes. Dinero didn't stop smiling, didn't stop talking to Wes, didn't stop passing him the ball. Sometimes it was like he went out of his way to make everybody else think that they were boys.

Wes knew better. They weren't. It was something he tried to explain to Emmanuel after their practice on Wednesday night, second-to-last one before their game at Montgomery County on Saturday.

"You're seeing things that aren't there," Emmanuel said. "Like you're seeing ghosts."

"He's not a ghost," Wes said. "He's right there with me on the court."

"He's not freezing you out," Emmanuel said. "You think I wouldn't notice?"

They were waiting for his mom to pick them up, where they were supposed to wait, in the front lobby.

"I'm trying to explain this to you without making it sound as if I have a big head," Wes said.

"You do have a big head, full of basketball," Emmanuel said. "But I know that's not the kind you mean."

Wes lowered his voice, even though the rest of the players were gone by now. But sometimes you said things that you were afraid *you* might hear.

"I should always be his first option," he said. "But I'm not. *That's* what I'm seeing."

"You're saying that if he doesn't give it to you when he should, it's the same as freezing you out."

"Exactly," Wes said. "He's the point guard. I get that he ought to have the ball more than me. But when we've scrimmaged the last two practices, he's giving me fewer touches. And there were even fewer tonight than there were on Monday."

"You're saying it's on account of what you said to him," Emmanuel said.

"Hundred percent."

"You're sure."

"You know what they say, E," Wes said. "Ball don't lie. And you know me well enough to know I never lie about ball."

It was little things, working themselves up to being big things. Dinero would wait just long enough after Wes got open so that by the time Wes got the ball, he was about to be covered close again. When they'd run the high pick-and-roll—a play that was money for them, like Dinero's nickname—Dinero was keeping it more.

And there were times when Wes shouldn't have gotten the ball, when he was all jammed up in traffic, that he did force it to him, even though there was no room for Wes to maneuver.

"He didn't like me telling him he was wrong," Wes said. "It's like nobody's allowed to do that with him."

"So, talk to him," Emmanuel said.

"Because that worked out so great the last time we got together?" Wes said. "All I did was make things worse."

"Sounds like it!"

He was smiling, though.

Emmanuel said, "Come on, he won't take this to the game. He wants to win the way we do."

Wes was sure he did. But only playing by his own rules.

The Dinero rules.

FOURTEEN

WES SOMETIMES THOUGHT—ACTUALLY A LOT of times thought—that his mom knew him as well as his dad knew basketball.

Like she knew him as a person the way his dad knew him as a player, even though Wes had always believed they were the same, you couldn't separate them even if you tried.

"Quiet tonight," she said at the end of dinner. "Something going on with the team?"

"Nothing I can't handle," he said.

"And it's something you can't talk to your old mom about?"

"It's a basketball thing."

"Ooooooooh," she said. "A basketball thing. Way above my motherly pay grade."

She winked at him.

"You know I didn't mean it that way," Wes said.

"Try me," she said. "If you're going too fast for me, I'll tell you."

"Funny," he said.

She sighed. "I know," she said.

So he told her. All of it. He told her about telling Dinero he was open right after the game. He told her about the one-on-one game and joking that he'd made the pass to himself that Dinero hadn't made. Told her about the way Dinero had reacted. And now the way he'd kept reacting at the Hawks' last two practices.

"You think he's getting in your way," she said, "jamming you up."

He nodded. "There's only five guys on a team," he said. "And all it takes for things to get out of whack is one." He shook his head. "And then things really *are* wack."

"Isn't he too good a player to let his ego get in the way of the team's goals?" she said.

"That's the way it ought to work."

"Not right now."

"Nope."

His mom said, "You obviously struck a nerve and hurt his feelings. So, apologize."

"I didn't do anything wrong," Wes said. "If there's anybody who should apologize, it's him. He's the one who made the bonehead play at the end of that game."

"I know you don't want to hear this," she said. "But you did call him out. Now, be the bigger man before this thing between the two of you jams up the whole team."

She smiled across the table at him.

"I know you're a guy. I know guys think that talking things out is against the law. But trust me, sometimes shutting up isn't the answer."

"Dad won't talk things out," he said.

"And look where that has gotten us," she said, in a sad voice that made Wes wish he'd known when to shut his big mouth.

He told her he'd think about it, but right now he had homework to do. His mom said to go ahead, she'd clean up, before pointing out that he often had homework he'd forgotten when he wanted to drop the subject.

He went upstairs, thinking he did want to talk things out, just not with Dinero. He wanted to talk things out with his dad. Who didn't talk about much of anything these days. He tried to call him when he got to his room, but it went straight to voice mail. It meant his phone was turned off again, or maybe it had died.

Wes texted him then, even knowing his dad never texted back.

But he had to try. His dad would know how to handle things with Dinero if he was here. Except that he wasn't here.

He actually did have homework to finish, for English and history. So he sat at his desk and finished all of it, forcing himself to concentrate, trying to keep his brain away from Dinero and basketball and his dad.

But everything was connected.

His dad had warned him about Dinero. In that way, his dad was the one still thinking one move ahead. But did that mean Dinero really was holding a grudge now, and he'd take that grudge to the next game?

Wes wouldn't know that until the next game.

What he decided was that he wasn't going to let his own ego get in the way of the team. He had been taught that nothing was more important than the team. If you elevated it, you elevated yourself in the process. Raise the team's game, raise your own. Simple as that. And you never put yourself ahead of the team. It always came back to the basics: Shoot if you were open, pass if somebody was more open. Have fun.

But he sure wasn't having fun right now, even though his team was 1–0.

So, he would have to work harder. He *was* going to be the best player he could be. He was going to show everybody who needed to be shown that he was ready for AAU ball next season.

And if he could do that, he told himself, there was no way his dad would want him to start on that journey without him. Even if his dad wasn't living at home, even as distant as he was—would he ever learn the reason why? Would his dad ever open up to him and his mom? He still could be a part of Wes's season. No way he would want to sit it out. It had to be why he was sneaking into Hawks' practices. It had to be why he'd come by the driveway so the two of them could talk. It was as if he were trying to come all the way back to Wes, but couldn't. Or wouldn't.

He shook his head hard to clear it, and wrote the last page of his Civil War paper, wondering if the best Union soldiers were the equivalent of Navy SEALs in olden days, wondering what they were like when they made it back home, if they made it back home.

These were his last two sentences:

"The only ones who knew how brave they were were the soldiers themselves. They saw what they saw fighting the war but stayed brave until their mission was accomplished."

He thought that was a pretty good ending.

Wes wanted a happy ending for himself, for his mom, for his dad. He saved his document, closed his laptop, brushed his teeth, gave one last check of his phone.

Nothing.

After his lights were off, his mom came in to say good night and tell him that she loved him. He said he loved her, too.

When he heard the door shut, he reached over and checked the phone again.

Still nothing.

For now, whatever he needed to figure out, he would have to figure out for himself. After all, he was Lt. Michael Davies's son. Now he was the one who had to be brave, at least in basketball, for both of them.

FIFTEEN

THERE WAS A LATE PRACTICE today, which worked out fine because this was Wes's day to meet with Mr. Correa after class, and take the late bus home.

Wes met with Mr. Correa more than once a week, sometimes popping into his office between classes. But if you had him as an adviser, you had to be on his calendar, usually on a set day. Today was that day.

Wes was glad. He knew what a great support system he still had, especially with his mom and Emmanuel. He had his team-mates, all of whom he liked, even if he liked Dinero Rey a lot less lately.

There was just something about Mr. Correa. Wes wasn't looking for some kind of substitute dad. Nobody was ever going to substitute for his real dad, even if he never changed all the way back into the person he used to be. Mr. Correa was like a grown-up friend. Or an older brother who was a *lot* older than Wes was.

"I'll always be here for you," Mr. Correa said to him one time, when Wes had first made him aware of what was going on with his dad.

"Here for what, though?" Wes said.

"Here for whatever you need me to be here for. And whenever you need me to be here."

So today, Wes thought, was a perfect day for whatever and whenever. And the whatever was what was going on between him and Dinero.

"Just gonna throw this out there," Mr. Correa said when Wes was across the desk from him, both of them once again surrounded by all those books. "But I'm guessing you're not here to talk about school."

"More like getting schooled," Wes said, "on the court."

"Explain," Mr. Correa said. "I got nothing but time."

Wes took his time, trying not to leave out any important parts, starting off from when Dinero had ignored him at the end of the game to take his hero shot, through their game of one-on-one, and what had been said between them at the end of *that* disaster. Then he told Mr. Correa about what he'd been seeing—and feeling—at practice since then.

"I know I probably sound crazed," Wes said. "But I'm not."

Mr. Correa grinned and raked his fingers through his long hair. Then he gave a quick scratch to the little growth of beard, which to Wes always looked to be the same length. It was all part of his look. Wes thought it was cool, the way Mr. Correa was.

"You're not crazy," Mr. Correa finally said.

"I'm not?" Wes said.

He laughed as soon as he did, realizing how relieved he sounded.

"Nope," Mr. Correa said.

Wes waited. He hadn't come here today expecting Mr. Correa to fix things for him. He just wanted somebody to understand him, not as a seventh-grader, not as someone apart from his own dad. Just as a basketball player. He wanted Mr. Correa to be his basketball adviser today, not his school adviser.

"One thing I'm sure you don't want to hear from me," Mr. Correa said, "is that these things have a way of working themselves out, right?"

"When my dad first came back home," Wes said, "and he started to act strangely, my mom told me that things would work out with him."

"Well, you got me there," Mr. Correa said. "Because the truth is, sometimes the big things don't work themselves out, even when you think they should."

Wes absently reached over, picked up the small orange Nerf basketball on the desk, turned, and shot it at the stand-up plastic basket in the corner, the basket set in place by the stacks of books on the floor around it.

Nothing but net.

"You always make that look easy," Mr. Correa said. "My shooting percentage from over here stinks."

"Something needs to be easy for me," Wes said.

"Good players on the same team have been working things out, at least eventually, since the beginning of time," his adviser said. "I could give you a long list of old players out of the past that you'd have to look up."

"None of them can help me out right now," Wes said.

"But their history can," Mr. Correa said. "Because what I'm

trying to give you here is a different kind of history class. Think of it as hoops history. Whether we're talking about American history or basketball history, the thing is, you can learn from it."

Wes said, "Is this another way of you telling me that this all is gonna work out?"

"Nope," Mr. Correa said. "I know that for all the stories about guys who did work it out, there are other stories about guys who didn't. And got themselves traded or became free agents or whatever."

"I don't think I'm eligible for free agency," Wes said.

Mr. Correa pointed a finger at him and smiled.

"And *sometimes*," he said, "there are guys who did figure it out and sort of un-figured it out, like LeBron and Kyrie."

Wes hadn't even thought about them, but he knew Mr. Correa was right, totally. LeBron and Kyrie had won a championship together with the Cavaliers, then made it back to the NBA Finals the next year. But then Kyrie Irving decided he didn't want to be in LeBron's shadow any longer, even though he didn't put it that way at the time. But he'd announced that he wanted to be traded, and now he was playing for the Celtics, where he was the man.

"Is that supposed to make me feel better?" Wes said.

"Nope," Mr. Correa said. "I'm trying to make you understand that if it gets this complicated for the biggest names in basketball, it can be *really* complicated for a couple of twelve-year-olds. We talk all the time about how LeBron is the greatest teammate in the world, but he turned out to not be great enough for Kyrie."

Mr. Correa came around the desk, picked up the Nerf ball, went back to his chair. Shot and missed.

"See what I mean," he said.

"About your poor shooting or LeBron and Kyrie?" Wes said.

"Both."

"But Kyrie was the one who asked to be traded."

"True. But I believe another reason was that he thought LeBron was going to be leaving after one more year."

"He does always sort of do what's best for himself," Wes said.

"It goes back to the thing about how sometimes great players are unselfish and selfish at the exact same time," Mr. Correa said.

"But what if I think Dinero is being more selfish than unselfish?" Wes said.

"Then there's a problem."

"Told you."

"What if I talk to him about this without saying that I talked to you about it?" Mr. Correa said. "Sound him out on how he thinks things are going with the Hawks, keeping it loose, and then see if he leaves me an opening to try to help you both out."

"No!" Wes said. "He'll know. And then he'll think I went running to you."

"You're right," his guidance counselor said. "As much as I'd like to make things right, the only two people who can do that are you and Dinero."

"But what if he likes things the way they are?"

"Then it will be more on you to let him see that they aren't, and that it will only hurt the team in the long run."

"Great," Wes said.

"Listen," Mr. Correa said, "from all that I do know about basketball history, when a couple of star hoopers get together, whether it was Durant and Westbrook or Durant and Steph or Westbrook and Paul George or LeBron and Kyrie, one has to give more than the other. You might not want to hear that, either. But it's true."

Now Wes got up, retrieved the orange ball, shot again.

Nothing but net, again.

"Glad this isn't a game of H-O-R-S-E," Mr. Correa said.

"I could give in a little with you and let you win," Wes said.

"Listen," Mr. Correa said. "I know enough about you to know that you're always going to do what's best for the team in the end. I know you're a bigger player than Dinero. So now you got to be the bigger man. So you can both play your best games."

"Not happening right now."

"Sounds like."

"Doesn't only sound like," Wes said. "That's the way it is."

"It *was* just one game," he said. "Maybe you could try talking to him again, maybe in a neutral setting, away from basketball."

Wes shook his head. "I've talked to him, I've talked to my mom, I've talked to Emmanuel about this. Now I've talked to you. I just want to play."

"So, keep playing your own game, as best you can," Mr. Correa said. He told Wes he'd try to come to one of the Hawks' next games to check out for himself what was going on.

"And you gotta keep something else in mind," Mr. Correa said. "There are more important things in your life right now than basketball."

He meant with his dad.

"I'm making up about as much ground with him," Wes said, "as I am with Dinero."

Joe Correa stood up now, nodded at the clock, and smiled.

"Things will get better," he said. "Maybe as soon as the next game."

They did not.

SIXTEEN

THEIR SECOND GAME WAS AGAINST the Montgomery County Grizzlies, in a really nice gym, at Bethesda-Chevy Chase High School, where the B-CC Barons played.

The place was a lot bigger than the Annapolis Rec Center, with *B-CC* painted in blue inside the free-throw lines and *Barons* painted in the same color on the floor behind the baskets. The seats in the bleachers were also blue.

"This is niiiiiiiice," Emmanuel Pike said when they were warming up.

"But the Grizzlies won't be nice," Wes said. "Remember, we're on the road, in a hostile arena."

Emmanuel whooped. "Hostile arena?" he said. "You really do watch way too much basketball on television."

"And that's a bad thing?" Wes said.

He knew a little about the Grizzlies, from Facebook and Insta. Mostly he knew that their best player was a small forward named Bakari Hogan, who'd scored thirty-two points in their opener against Potomac Valley.

Wes had managed to find a box score online, from one of the

local newspapers, and saw that no one else on the Grizzlies had even been in double figures.

He watched Bakari going through his own warmups at the other end of the court, long dreadlocks hanging all the way to his shoulders, pulled together in a ponytail back then. He wore a cool black sleeve on his shooting arm, and high black socks that Wes thought went great with the Grizzlies' black-and-navy-blue uniforms. Total dude.

"You think I could ever rock hair like that?" Emmanuel said.

"No," Wes said.

"You're saying I can't style?"

"Your styling is not trying to style," Wes said. "It's why we're like brothers."

"In a hostile arena," E said.

Wes grinned. "Glad that you remembered," he said.

They had gone through their layup drills, and were getting ready to just shoot around. Dinero came walking over to them. He hadn't been ignoring Wes today. Wes hadn't been ignoring him. They'd said hi to each other when they'd both shown up. Nothing much beyond that. What chirp and chatter there had been from Dinero in the layup line had been directed at Josh and Russ Adams and DeAndre. And Emmanuel. Pretty much everybody except Wes.

Wes imagined them as a couple of cars traveling in different lanes.

Just as long as they didn't start heading right for each other, on another collision course.

"Better have your big-boy pants on today, Number Thirteen," Dinero said. "'Cause I hear that this Bakari can really ball."

Wes stepped back, smiling so that Dinero could see he was just playing and pulled up his own shorts as high as they would go.

"I hear he wants to put it to you good," Dinero said.

"Who told you that?" Emmanuel said.

"I got my sources," Dinero said.

Now he smiled.

"Just giving you a big heads-up," Dinero said to Wes.

"It's up," Wes said.

Dinero laughed. "Make sure it's not up you-know-where."

Dinero, still smiling, ran over and picked up a loose ball and dribbled it toward the corner, behind his back, through his legs, then drained a jumper, as if he assumed Wes was still watching him.

Wes *was* watching him, wondering whether their game-within-the-game had started already.

Or if it ever really ended.

Bakari Hogan, the dude with the high socks and the hair and the shooting sleeve, turned out to be an expression that Emmanuel used all the time:

He was *allthat.*

One word, not two.

He could run the court and pass like a champ, because he could *see* the court. That meant all of it, all the time. The Grizzlies' guards weren't much, especially their point guard, a kid named Sammy Wilder. Their secondary scorer, and second-best player, was their center, a kid named Bo, with whom Bakari played a two-man game when he wasn't being a one-man show.

When Bakari wasn't showing off all his mad skills, he preferred running the Grizzlies' offense off high picks from Bo, the biggest player in the game. DeAndre couldn't handle Bo. Neither could Emmanuel, when Coach Saunders switched him over to center late in the first quarter.

But even with all the good things Bakari and Bo were doing, the Hawks were staying even with them. Wes made two straight threes, after not having seen the ball much before that. The Hawks' offense sure wasn't running through him the way it was for Bakari at the other end. At least he had managed to get on the board.

And he honestly hadn't been all that concerned about not getting the ball before he made those two bombs, for the simple reason that Dinero was killing it on offense.

Killing. It.

It didn't matter who the Grizzlies' coach matched up on him. There were even a couple of times when he had Bakari try. Didn't help. Dinero was just on today, even making his outside shots. When somebody would get up on him outside, he'd drive past them, either score himself or dish to Emmanuel or DeAndre.

Dinero had clearly made up his mind, once he determined that they couldn't guard him, that the matchup that mattered today wasn't Wes and Bakari. It was Bakari and him. One time, after Dinero had beaten Sammy, their point guard, again and gotten a layup, he didn't look back at Sammy. He looked over at Bakari and smiled and shook his head. Wes wasn't even sure if Bakari caught it. Wes did.

It was as if he were saying:

Not your gym.

Mine.

By the end of the first quarter it was Hawks 20, Grizzlies 18. Wes looked up at the big scoreboard above their basket and wondered if more points would be scored in one quarter in their league all season. Other than his two baskets, and a couple of layups from E and DeAndre, the rest of their scoring had come from Dinero.

But Coach decided to give him a rest at the start of the second quarter. When he told Josh to go in for him, Dinero blurted out, "But, Coach!"

Coach calmly turned and gave him a long look and said, "Exactly, I'm the coach. You can wait until I call your number again in a couple of minutes."

Dinero opened his mouth, then closed it. Finally he said, "Yes, sir."

Coach left Wes out there for now. As Wes started to walk back on the court to join his teammates, Coach walked with him and said, "Let's put the ball in your hands a little more. And make that talented young fella work a little harder at our end."

And it worked.

Josh, in at point guard, was happy to let Wes take the lead. It was Josh's way of being a team guy. Because as the Hawks quickly stretched *their* lead, everybody could see Coach's new game plan was working. And Josh wasn't going to let his ego get in that way of that.

My kind of player, Wes thought.

Wes was moving the ball around, getting everybody else involved, E and DeAndre and Josh and Russ. Over the first three minutes of the quarter, the Hawks went on a 10–2 run, and everybody on the court for the Hawks had one basket. A couple of times Wes looked over to the scorer's table, expecting to see Dinero there, getting ready to check back in.

He was still sitting next to Coach.

But Wes couldn't worry about him. He was too busy playing, happy to be playing the way he was and the way the Hawks were. It was 34–24 when Dinero finally did check back in, replacing Josh. Coach gave Wes a rest, too.

There were two minutes left, the Hawks still ahead by six points, when Wes checked back in.

He didn't touch the ball the rest of the half. There were two Hawks' possessions when no one except Dinero touched the ball. He brought it up, dribbled around until he was ready to make his move. Once he pulled up and made a jumper. The other time he got in too deep on a drive and missed a layup. It was as if the Hawks had been one team when he'd been on the bench and were a totally different team now.

But when he banked in a three-pointer to beat the horn, getting the Hawks' lead back up to five, he ran off the court as if he were on his way to cut down the nets, even though there was still an entire half left to play.

Wes watched him and thought:

How can somebody this good be this bad at understanding team ball?

But Dinero came running over to him and said, "We got this!" and put up his hand for a high five. Wes gave him one back, wondering if he meant that their team had this.

Or just the Money Man.

In the second half, Wes made it his mission to stop Bakari as best he could, or at least slow him down. Do as much as he could on defense to help his team win the game. He dogged Bakari all over the court, tried to move him off his favorite spots, boxed out aggressively to keep Bakari off the boards. He was basically doing so many of the things he'd been taught to do his whole life, the kind of things that never ended up in a box score, but helped you win.

Unfortunately, Bakari's size began to take its toll on Wes, who found himself committing three fouls before the half was halfway over. He would have to be more careful.

On offense, Coach had told Dinero to move the ball around, actually told him to be a little less of a ball stopper. Dinero nodded as if he understood. Yet it still seemed to Wes that Dinero was only passing him the ball as a last resort. Wes told himself not to force things when Dinero did, to stay within the offense. He got two more baskets in the middle of the quarter, one on a putback, the other on a neat drive past Bakari, who reached in, causing a foul of his own. Wes made the free throw for a three-point play.

The game was tied going into the fourth quarter. Both starting fives back out there. Dinero really had dialed down hogging the ball now, especially with the Grizzlies having switched to a zone defense. But even with that, at least to Wes's eyes, Dinero was still trying to impress Bakari. He wanted his eyes on him the way he wanted everybody's eyes in the gym on him.

Hey, look at me.

Two straight times, with under four minutes left to play, game tied both times, Dinero ignored the fact that Wes was open because he was lost in one of his shake-and-bake moves, like the announcers said, once with Bakari covering him on a switch.

Dinero missed both of the shots he ended up hoisting.

During a timeout with two minutes to go, Hawks down a basket by now, Coach said, "I don't care who shoots it at the end of this possession. But I want everybody to touch the ball. Am I clear?"

They all nodded, Dinero included.

They ran their motion offense. Everybody got at least one touch. E finally cleaned out Bakari with a hard, legal screen. Josh threw Wes the ball, and he squared up and hit a jumper. Hawks up a point, 54–53.

Wes hounded Bakari into a miss at the other end, managing to avoid a foul. E got the rebound and hit Wes with a smooth outlet pass. He had space in front of him and had Bakari beat. But he saw Dinero streaking down the left side, ahead of everybody. Wes threw him a perfect bounce pass; Dinero got a layup. Now the Hawks were up three.

The Grizzlies quickly got the ball back in Bakari's hands. Even with Wes's hand in his face, Bakari made a jumper just inside the three-point line. Both teams feeling it now.

Hawks still up by one. One minute left.

Now Dinero held the ball too long again, as if everybody getting a touch had only applied to the Hawks' last possession. Wes ran the baseline twice, right to left, left to right, and shook free from Bakari finally. Dinero ignored him, forcing the ball to the middle, where he took an off-balance shot that missed.

Bakari had the rebound and pushed the ball, played his two-man game with Bo. Bo made a baby hook.

The lead gone. Grizzlies by one.

Ten seconds left.

Coach yelled, "Ohio."

One of Wes's favorite plays. E set a weak-side screen for him. Wes cut for the basket as soon as he did. If he wasn't open, he kept right on going, to the right corner. Coach knew the way everybody on the team knew that it was one of Wes's sweet spots.

Clearly Coach was going to give him the chance to win the game.

E came up the way he was supposed to. But Bakari blew up the play, giving ground before E even had a chance to set the screen. Wes ran for the basket anyway, Bakari with him step for step. Wes knew he had the edge, because he knew what was going to happen next even if Bakari didn't, that he was about to make a hard right turn for the corner. Wes was sure it would give him all the opening he needed.

Dinero still had the ball at the top of the key.

Bakari was on Wes's shoulder as the two of them approached the basket.

Now.

Two things happened then, pretty much at the exact same moment, hard to tell which happened first, neither one good for the Annapolis Hawks.

Wes made his cut.

Dinero threw the ball right where he'd been.

The pass went out of bounds, behind Wes, with three seconds showing on the clock.

Grizzlies' ball.

The Hawks never even got the chance to foul. Bakari quickly took the ball from the ref, threw a half-court pass to Bo, who dribbled out the clock. And the game.

As soon as the horn sounded, Dinero walked straight for Wes, and in a voice only the two of them could hear said, "I passed you the ball this time. You happy?"

"I wasn't open," Wes said.

"Then maybe I should get the ball to someone who is next time."

Before Dinero walked away, he said one more thing under his breath.

Told Wes that his head had ended up you-know-where after all.

SEVENTEEN

ONLY WES HEARD WHAT DINERO said.

And the first thing that hit Wes, even more than the hurt of what had just happened, was this:

What if Dinero was right?

Not about Wes playing with his head up his you-know-what. But had Wes been playing with his head *down*? Had he been open enough for Dinero to get him the ball?

So as mean as Dinero had sounded, as mean as a toothache, maybe he *was* right. Maybe Wes had done the one thing you were never supposed to do on a basketball court, and had lost sight of where the ball was.

And now the Hawks had lost a game because of that.

Wes's mom had made the trip to Bethesda for the game. When Wes was out of the handshake line, and Coach had actually told all of the players on his team to keep their heads up, Christine Davies came over and reminded Wes that he was going home with Mr. and Mrs. Pike and Emmanuel, because she had to get right back to the book fair that had started today at Annapolis High, and would go on all week. She also reminded him that she would be home in plenty of time to make them dinner.

"You played beautifully," his mom said.

"Mom," he said. "We lost."

"Not your fault," she said.

"You sure about that?"

She gave him a quick kiss on the cheek and got close to his ear and said, "That pass didn't throw itself away."

And left.

Emmanuel Pike knew enough to know that Wes had no interest in talking about the game on the ride home and must have told his parents not to talk about it, either. So they didn't, mostly riding in silence all the way back to Annapolis.

When they pulled up to Wes's house, E said, "You want me to come in and we'll just hang for a while?"

"I can come pick up Emmanuel later," E's mom said.

"No thanks, I'll call you later," Wes said. "Nobody wants to hang with me right now."

"I do," E said.

"Call you later," Wes said again.

"You're just gonna go inside and keep blaming yourself for a loss that wasn't your fault, right?" E said.

"Basically, yeah," Wes said.

"Figured so," Emmanuel said.

"You know me," Wes said.

"Aw, man, do I ever?" Emmanuel Pike said.

Wes didn't notice his dad sitting on the front step, back against the front door, until Mr. Pike had backed out of the driveway, and their car had pulled away.

EIGHTEEN

THERE WAS NO CAR AROUND. Once again, his dad had managed to show up when his mom wasn't here. But how did he know that? If they'd been talking in the last couple of days, Wes was sure his mom would have said something about that. But she hadn't.

Did his dad know she was at the book fair? But if he knew, how did he?

Or did he not care?

"Hey, Dad," Wes said.

He had his bag over his shoulder. He'd changed into his street sneakers after the game, so his game shoes were in the bag, along with a bottle of water and the shooting shirt all the Hawks wore during warmups.

"Hey, kid," Michael Davies said.

He was wearing his old Orioles cap and what looked to be the same old jeans he'd worn on his last visit, and a dark blue Navy hoodie.

"Mom's not here," Wes said. "She's over at school."

His dad nodded, not saying whether that was news to him

or not. To Wes, he looked even more tired than usual and even thinner.

And older, somehow.

"We lost today," Wes said.

"How'd you play?"

"Pretty well, until the very end," Wes said, and then he described the last play. How he thought he was covered. How Dinero threw the ball to him anyway. How Dinero had hogged the ball for most of the game, until that moment.

When he finished, his dad said, "Well, you win some, you lose some."

He got up now, slowly, and Wes thought he might want to go inside. But all he did was sit back down on the top step of the front stoop.

Wes thought, You win some, you lose some?

"I kind of feel like the turnover was as much my fault as his," Wes said. "Maybe more."

His dad actually laughed.

What was so funny?

"Did he really say that about getting your head out of your rear end?" Michael Davies said.

"He didn't say rear end," Wes said.

"Gotta admit," his dad said, "sounds like a pretty good analysis, if you ask me. But don't you worry. One day that boy's going to hang a poster of you on his wall. He's lucky he gets to share the same court with you." Then he laughed again.

Wes's whole life, every game that he'd ever played when his dad was around, they'd broken down the game when it was over, as if Wes were still trying to break down a defense. If his dad had attended the game, he'd focus on the parts he thought were most important. If he hadn't been there, Wes would be the one to pick out the highlights and lowlights, almost as if he were playing the big moments of the game all over again.

Wes wanted that today, in the worst way. He wanted him to be that dad, one more time.

Only this dad was the one acting as if his head weren't in the game.

"You feeling okay, Dad?" he said.

"Never better," he said brightly. "Why do you ask?"

"You're just acting a little funny, is all."

"What, a guy can't be funny? Lighten your load a little there, big guy. It's a long season." Now he had this goofy grin on his face. "It's just one game, for crying out loud."

"You used to tell me that they're all big games if somebody is keeping score," Wes said.

There was no indication that his dad had heard what he just said. Or maybe he'd heard and just didn't care.

"You got any water?" his dad said now. "Little thirsty all of a sudden."

Wes said he did, reached into his bag and handed the bottle in there, one he hadn't opened yet, to his dad, who took it and seemed to drink half of the water down in loud gulps.

When he was finished, he set it down carefully beside him, almost as if he were afraid that somehow the plastic bottle might break if he tipped it over.

"I actually think things between me and Dinero are getting

worse," Wes said, trying to get the subject back to basketball.

His dad lifted his shoulders, let them fall. "Still early," he said.

Neither one of them spoke now.

Finally Wes said, "You staying for dinner tonight?"

In his head, he thought that if he could just get him to stick around, as weirdly as he was acting, it would feel as if he'd won something today.

"Gotta be someplace," his dad said. The goofy grin again. "And you know what they say, right? Everybody's gotta be somewhere."

"Okay," Wes said, and then almost by reflex said, "Maybe next time."

Suddenly there was the sound of his mom's car pulling into the driveway. It seemed to startle his dad, the grin disappearing from his face, his eyes wide. He seemed to lean away from the noise of the car engine, and as he did, he knocked over the water bottle, the rest of its contents spilling across the top step.

By now his mom was out of the car, closing the door, but not making any move toward the house. She was just staring at Wes's dad.

"Michael," she said.

He spread out his arms and said, "Honey, I'm home!"

She looked in the direction of the street. "Where's your car?"

"Took an Uber," he said.

She nodded.

"And why was that?" she said.

"I do that sometimes when I don't feel like driving," he said. The grin was back. "Just sit back and enjoy the ride."

"I've asked you to call before you stop by," she said. "It's the polite and respectful thing to do. For Wes and for me."

He put his arms out wide, palms up. "Forgot my manners," he said. "My bad."

"You're welcome to stay," she said. "I've got enough food for three."

"Thanks but no thanks," he said. "I'll just walk for a while and then Uber on home."

Christine Davies said, "Let me drive you."

"No need."

"I'd be happy to do it."

Wes's head was going back and forth, from his mom to his dad. It was like some kind of standoff, even with his dad still sitting down.

"Nah," he said. "Adios, amigos."

He waved. Wes's mom started up the walk as his dad started down it. He tried to give her a lot of room to pass him, actually moving over so that he was on the lawn. But she stopped suddenly and got in front of him, blocking his way.

They were almost nose to nose. Neither one of them spoke until Wes's mom said, "Your breath."

He watched as his dad broke the stare-down and just looked down now. When he tried to move around her again, she blocked his way again, almost as if she were guarding him.

"Please," he said.

Michael Davies looked back up at his wife, then at Wes, then back at her.

"Not in front of the boy," he said in a voice that wasn't much more than a whisper.

"Please don't," he said. "Just let me go."

But Wes knew there was no stopping her now.

"Don't you ever come to this house again after you've been drinking," she said.

His dad hung his head a little and shuffled his feet.

Then she let him pass. Wes and his mom watched him slowly walk toward the street. When he got to the sidewalk, he seemed uncertain about which way to go, finally made up his mind, and went left.

Wes thought for a second about going after him, even took a step in his direction before he stopped.

"Let him go," she said.

She walked into the house without looking back. Wes followed her, stopping only long enough to reach down and pick up the empty water bottle.

NINETEEN

WES AND HIS MOM WERE sitting in the den where he had once watched basketball with his dad.

His mom had made herself a cup of tea. Wes was having hot chocolate. As much as he liked hot chocolate, he knew it never made things better. But it sure never made them worse.

"I've seen him like this before," Wes's mom said in a sad voice, with sad eyes to go along with it. "But I never thought he'd let you see him this way."

"He wasn't that bad," Wes said. "As weird as he was acting, he actually seemed kind of happy. He even laughed."

"They call them happy drunks," she said.

She had her big mug in both hands and drank some of her tea. There was, Wes saw, still steam coming off it.

Wes said, "I can't remember the last time I heard Dad laugh."

"I just wish it came out of him, and not a bottle," she said.

"Was he really drunk?" Wes said.

It had occurred to him as they were having their conversation that he didn't really know what a person who was drunk acted like. He knew he had never seen his dad like this, even if he didn't know what was causing him to act the way he was.

"I don't think he was all the way drunk," Wes's mom said. "And I don't really think he was happy. I think he drinks not to be sad. And that may make trick him into thinking he is happy. But he's not."

Her eyes were so big and sad now Wes was afraid she might cry. As much as he hated to see his dad in pain, he hated it just as much when his mom cried. It was her way of telling Wes how much pain she was in, too.

And he felt as helpless with her as he did with his dad.

"We can only control what we can control," she said.

Wes thought, she sounds like Dad talking about basketball.

"No," she continued, "let me rephrase that. We can only do what he allows us to do. In the end, the only person who can make your father happy again is your father."

"So you're saying we shouldn't even try?"

He was never going to stop trying, not with basketball, not with his dad.

"No," his mom said, "I'm not saying that at all. I will never give up on him. I know that's not the way you're wired, either. But I've learned the hard way that we can't help him if he won't make the effort to help himself."

"Isn't there some kind of doctor who can help him?" Wes said.

"He was seeing someone at the academy," she said. "But he stopped going. He'd rather go to the bar these days."

"But he came here."

"Probably from the bar," she said.

"Doesn't that count for something?"

"He still wants to connect with you, honey," she said. "He wants to do that in the worst way. The problem is that today he did it in the worst way."

"So why did he come?"

"I think he's afraid of losing you. It's probably why he had a few drinks. To get his courage up."

"But he's the bravest person I know," Wes said.

"This isn't about courage in the face of the enemy," she said. "Because right now your father's worst enemy is himself."

He didn't know what to say. He didn't know what to do. His mom talked about controlling what you could control. The only time Wes felt in control right now is when he had a basketball in his hands, even if it wasn't in his hands as often as he wanted it to be. As crazy as it might sound if he tried to explain it to his mom, he still had the same plan:

Get better at basketball, get his dad back.

All he had.

His mom reached down now, carefully set her mug on the coaster in front of her on the coffee table. She had been sitting in a chair across from the couch where Wes was. Now she came around the table and sat next to him.

"Sweetheart," she said. "Have you ever heard of post-traumatic stress disorder? Sometimes people just call it by its initials: PTSD."

Wes thought it sounded like something they were always trying to cure with medicine on television commercials. Every time

Wes would see one of those commercials, he'd wonder whether there was something his dad could take to get better.

He told his mom that he might have heard something about it watching the new SEALs show on television.

"It's something that can affect people when they come back from fighting a war," she said. "Doesn't just affect them, but changes them. They come back and they're angry all the time. Or they can't hold a job. Or they get set off by the littlest thing that reminds them of war. All of a sudden they're not the same person they used to be."

"Like Dad is right now," Wes said.

"Yes," she said. "Sometimes it's something that happened to them. Or to someone they cared about. Or both. But when they get back home, even when they're one of the lucky ones who *did* make it back home, they can't let go of whatever put them in a bad place in the first place. It's like the war and all the bad memories that go with it have followed them all the way home."

"But you can get better from it, right?" Wes asked her.

He wanted her to say yes right away, as if that was the easiest and most obvious answer in the world. But she did not.

"I told you that I would never lie to you, so I'm not going to start now," she said. "Some people do get better. Many people get better. Just not all."

"But Dad's not just brave, he's strong," Wes said.

And just like that, she finally started to cry. But instead of wiping the tears away, she reached across the couch and put her hand over Wes's.

"PTSD can make even a strong man like your father weak," she said.

"But we still don't know what the thing was," Wes said.

"Maybe," she said, "it wasn't just one thing, it was everything."

"And now it's followed Dad home," Wes said.

The tears kept rolling down her cheek. She wouldn't let go of Wes's hand.

"I'm sorry that today he brought them to this home," she said.

Wes wanted to be strong now for his mom. He just didn't know how. It was clear that there was nothing left for them to say, so he said he was going to grab his basketball.

Sometimes that ball felt like a life preserver.

TWENTY

THERE WAS AN OPEN GYM, and good games, at the rec center on Sunday afternoons between noon and two o'clock. Wes asked his mom after church if she would drive him over there.

She said, "Have you ever considered that a basketball-free day might be a good thing once in a while?"

"No," he said.

"Will you know anybody who'll be playing there?" she said.

"It might be fun for a change *not* to know anybody in the game."

"Won't a lot of the boys be older?"

Wes smiled at her. It might have been the first smile he felt coming over him since yesterday's game had ended the way it had.

"The better the competition, the better you play," Wes said.

"Silly me," she said, smiling back. "How could I have forgotten a basketball fact of life like *that*?"

"You've got a lot on your plate," he said.

"Don't we all."

She dropped him off a few minutes after noon. There were already games being played on all three courts. It gave Wes a chance to look around, check out the level of play, see which game might be the best fit for him. But he didn't have to look for long because he saw Mr. Correa in a game on the court closest to the front doors.

When Mr. Correa noticed Wes to the side, he held up one finger. It turned out his game was one basket away from being over. He scored it, beating his man cleanly on a drive. As soon as he did, he jogged over to where Wes was standing.

"I'm going to use my excellent powers of observation and assume you're looking for a game," he said.

"Kind of."

"Couple of my buds are leaving," Mr. Correa said, "to go watch football. But the rest of the guys are hard-core and want to keep going."

"You think I'm good enough?"

"As a matter of fact, I do!" Mr. Correa said.

"How serious?" Wes asked.

"Just serious fun," Joe Correa said.

Wes was nervous, but it was the kind of nervous that could make you raise the level of your game the same as the competition could. There were four guys who looked to be about Mr. Correa's age, a couple of eighth-graders, two high school seniors that Mr. Correa told Wes had been the last two cuts at Annapolis High, and were going to try out again this season.

Mr. Correa introduced Wes around, told them that he was one of the stars of the Hawks.

"Don't listen to him," Wes said.

"They have to listen," Mr. Correa said. "I'm a teacher."

One of the older guys said, "Not my teacher."

"I can tell by the way you play," Mr. Correa said.

One of the high school kids, Neil, was on their team. So was one of the eighth-graders, Rakeem, tall for his age, who said he'd be playing on the team from St. Anne's of Annapolis this season. The other two players on their side were Mr. Correa and his friend, Chuck Giles, who Rakeem said was his English teacher at St. Anne's.

"Wes," Mr. Correa said, "why don't you play point? Chuck and I will play their bigs. Rakeem can play in the backcourt with you while Neil plays up front with Chuck and me."

"Mr. Correa, you know I don't play point for the Hawks, right? Dinero does."

"Yeah," he said, "but we both know there's a point guard inside you just *begging* to bust out."

As they walked out on the court Wes whispered to Mr. Correa, "I'm the youngest guy here."

Mr. Correa gave him a pat on the back.

"You're not here to get your lifeguard certificate," he said. "Just to play some ball."

The kid guarding Wes, with long blond hair and long arms and legs, was also an eighth-grader from St. Anne's. His name was Troy Sutherland. He said he'd probably be playing for St. Anne's this season, too.

Before they started he said to Wes, "How're things working out with you and Dinero?"

"How do you know about me and Dinero?" Wes said.

Troy laughed. "Are you kidding? Everybody in town does. So, is he giving you enough touches?"

"Only if I take him for ice cream," Wes said.

Wes didn't play good nervous at the start. Just nervous. He was too conscious about passing the ball first chance he got, not trying to make anything happen himself, never looking for his own shot. They were playing to twenty baskets, because there were no players right now waiting to play winners.

The score was 5–5, side out for Wes's team, when Mr. Correa came over to him.

"Start playing your game," he said, "and not the one you think you should be playing."

He started to say something, but Mr. Correa was already walking away, just adding this over his shoulder:

"Your ball today."

As Wes dribbled the ball toward the top of the circle, he made eye contact with Mr. Correa and gave him a nod. Mr. Correa immediately came running up and set a screen on Troy, creating space for Wes, who drove to the right. The guy guarding Mr. Correa slid over to cut him off. Wes went up in the air, as if he were about to attempt a short jumper anyway. Even elevated like it was a jump shot. But at the last second he saw that Mr. Correa had seen the opening for him that the switch had created and was flashing to the basket.

Wes sold his shooting motion right until the last second, when he fired a pass to Mr. Correa, who caught the ball and laid it in.

As they headed back up the court, Wes said to Mr. Correa, "My first career assist to a teacher."

And gave him a fast hand slap.

Troy brought the ball up. Wes played off him a bit, trying to read his eyes, because he'd noticed Troy mostly passed the ball where he was looking. So Wes sat back in a passing lane as Mr. Correa's man, Pete, came running up to the wing. Now Troy really was like a quarterback whose eyes had locked on his primary receiver. As he looped the ball in the direction of Pete, Wes made his move, stepping in, intercepting the ball easily. Wes probably could have driven the length of the court and scored easily himself, but Rakeem had taken off as soon as Wes had stepped in on the pass. Wes hit Rakeem with a long, perfect bounce pass, and Rakeem laid the ball in with a flourish, turning the play into a reverse even though there was nobody close to him. Just for the serious fun of it.

He heard about it right away from just about everybody in the game.

"Wasn't just mustard on that hot dog," his teacher, Mr. Giles, said. "Was relish and sauerkraut, too."

"More like hot sausage, if you ask me," Mr. Correa said.

Rakeem, grinning, ducked his head in embarrassment. "Okay," he said. "Okay, I get it. Can't a brother style a little bit?"

The other players yelled, *"No!"*

Sometimes Wes would let Rakeem bring the ball up, and get them into their offense. Or Neil. Or Mr. Correa. It was because sharing the ball was easy today. If he gave it up, he didn't have to worry that he wasn't going to see it again on that possession.

Wes felt free today, almost lighter than normal, as if he'd stopped carrying so much stuff around with him.

This was ball the way it was supposed to be. Maybe, he thought, the real reason he'd had his head down in a big moment yesterday was because he had been spending so much time lately walking around with his head down.

Yesterday wasn't him.

Today was.

At 14–all he got too fancy with a pass to Mr. Correa, maybe styling a little bit himself, and threw the ball behind him and out of bounds. But as bad as the pass was, he was able to laugh at himself.

In mock outrage, Mr. Correa said, "You think any of this is *funny*, Mr. Davies?"

Like they were in school.

"Kind of," Wes said.

"Yeah," Mr. Correa said. "Me too."

They got to 19–19 when Wes, in traffic, managed to bank in a floater. Best shot he'd made all day. Then Troy threw the ball away at the other end.

Their ball now, with a chance to win.

Wes brought it up. Without anybody telling them to, his teammates spread the court. Rakeem ended up in the left corner, Mr. Correa in the right. Neil came out. Wes passed it to him. Neil passed it back. When the ball was in Wes's hands, he saw Rakeem running hard down the baseline from the left, Mr. Correa from the right.

Neither one was looking to set a pick.

They were both just doing what you were supposed to:

Filling empty spaces.

Wes was eyeballing Rakeem. But it was Mr. Correa who got open. Wes saw that with his basketball eyes. And as soon as Mr. Correa was looking—playing with *his* head up—Wes whipped him a fierce chest pass.

Mr. Correa caught the ball, squared up, shot, made it, ball game.

Mr. Giles came over and said to Wes, "Are you certain you're only twelve years old?"

"Positive."

Mr. Giles high-fived him. So did the other players on their team. Mr. Correa was last.

"You played big today," he said to Wes.

"Bigger than I felt when I showed up," he said.

"Bigger and older," Mr. Correa said.

"Sometimes you make your team better and sometimes your team makes you better," Wes said.

"And sometimes," his adviser said, "it's a little bit of both."

Mr. Correa said that was the last game for him, he wanted to watch some football on television, too. Wes said he was done as well, he was going to end on a high note. Mr. Correa said he could drop Wes at home, as a way of saving his mom a trip. Wes went over to his bag and grabbed his phone and told her what Mr. Correa had said.

She said, fine with her, things were crazy at the book fair this afternoon. Wes said, "But that's a good thing, right?"

"Any school librarian in this world," she said, "would tell you it's actually a great thing."

She said she'd see him at home. Before she ended the call, she asked if open gym had been a good thing.

"A great thing," Wes said.

Mr. Correa asked him then how he planned to celebrate the way he'd just run with the big dogs.

"By asking you to make a stop on the way home," Wes said.

"Where we going?" Mr. Correa said.

"To my dad's place," Wes said.

TWENTY-ONE

WES KNEW HIS DAD LIVED at the Woodside Garden Apartments on Newtowne Drive. But he had never been there, not even with his mom.

His mom had told him on the phone that she didn't think Wes going over there was a good idea. He told her he really wanted to do it. They went back and forth for a couple of minutes like they were passing a ball before she finally said, "I don't want you to allow your father to think that yesterday was okay, no matter what he's going through. Because it was not okay."

"Okay," Wes said.

"I mean it, Wesley," she said.

Wesley. Always meant business, even when she didn't change her tone of voice.

"Not saying it was okay," Wes said to her. "I only want him to know that just because he had a bad day that I'm not giving up on him or anything."

"They're all bad days these days."

"So maybe I can make this a good one," Wes said. "Or at least a better one."

He asked her then for his dad's apartment number. She gave it to him. She said that if his dad wasn't there, Mr. Correa should bring Wes straight home, that she didn't want Wes to go looking for his father.

"I wouldn't even know where to look," Wes said.

"I would," his mom said.

The Woodside Garden Apartments were a bunch of redbrick buildings that all looked the same to Wes. From the parking lot where Mr. Correa pulled in they could see a big lawn in the middle of some of the buildings that was more brown than green, separated by a series of black iron fences. Somehow the place made Wes think of a prison. And maybe it was a kind of prison for his dad, who more and more, at least to Wes, seemed trapped by his own sad life.

Wes stood in front of the first-floor apartment where he knew his dad lived. Mr. Correa said he'd wait in the car. Wes saw his dad's car parked in the space that had the number of his apartment painted on it. Wes told Mr. Correa that since his dad was here, he didn't have to wait, his dad could probably drive him home.

But on the way over, Wes told Mr. Correa what had happened at the house the day before and how his mom had called out his dad for drinking.

"I got no place to be," Joe Correa said. "If you end up deciding you want to stay awhile, come back out, and we'll figure something out."

Wes walked up the short walk and stood in front of the door. The front drapes were closed. He wondered if his dad might somehow be peeking through them and could see him standing in front of the door.

Man, Wes thought, when did it get this hard just to see my own dad?

When did everything in his life that had once been so easy get this hard?

He rang the bell and waited.

Nothing.

Maybe his dad had gone for another of his walks. Maybe he *had* gone to a bar—even though it was still pretty early on a Sunday afternoon—to drink and maybe watch the Ravens' game on television. Before his dad had shown up at the house yesterday, Wes would never have thought of him going to a bar during the day.

He did now.

Rang the buzzer again.

Nothing.

Crickets, as his mom liked to say.

Would he really not answer the door if he knew Wes was out here?

Wes started to bang on the door then, and then kept banging, hitting it harder and harder with his right fist, not worrying that he was doing that with his shooting hand.

In that moment all the anger that had been building inside him, the anger about so many things going on in his life right now, came out of him.

Wes didn't care if anybody else at the Woodside Garden Apartments was watching him or could hear the racket he was making.

He wanted to hit something and keep hitting.

Before long he had his hands over his head, balled into fists, and was pounding with both of them, and would have kept doing that except somebody grabbed his hands from behind, freezing them over his head.

For a second he thought it might be his dad, maybe coming home from wherever he'd been.

Wes twisted around and saw that it was Mr. Correa, who said in a soft voice, "Let's take you home."

TWENTY-TWO

"I JUST KNOW HE WAS IN there," Wes said to his mom.

He didn't tell her about the way he'd pounded on the door or the way Mr. Correa had finally stopped him. Neither did Mr. Correa.

"But if he was in there," Wes said, "why wouldn't he answer the door?"

"Because he was afraid," she said.

When he'd first come home, he'd only gone in the house long enough to get his basketball. At least he could go outside and pound that without hurting himself. Or feeling more hurt than he already did.

He knew he should have been basketballed out. But he wasn't. Once he was outside, dribbling the ball, shooting it, he began to feel as if he could breathe normally again.

It was having the ball in his hands.

One ball.

His.

He was at least in control of that. He was in control of something, at least for a little while.

When he was back inside, he sat down at the kitchen table while his mom prepared dinner, one of his favorites, her world-class lasagna. She had been in the shower when he first got home. This was the first chance they'd gotten to talk about what had happened at the Woodside Garden Apartments.

"So you're saying that even today he was afraid to see me because of what happened yesterday?" Wes said.

She turned to face him.

"He's not just afraid of you," she said. "He's afraid of everything right now, everything that's outside once he opens that door."

She let out a big sigh. He was afraid that she might start crying. Right now, Wes was the one afraid. Of that.

"He's afraid of *life*," she said, "probably because of all the death and dying he saw over there."

"I know I keep telling you this," Wes said, "but we've got to find out what happened."

"And I keep telling *you*," she said, "that putting more pressure on him isn't going to help. I've talked to a lot of people about this. They believe that him wanting to tell us will be the beginning of him helping himself."

She smiled, but even doing that seemed to tire her out. Usually she loved having Wes in the kitchen with her while she cooked, him telling her about his day at school, her telling Wes not to leave anything out. He'd say that a lot of it was boring. She'd say that was impossible, to forget about that commercial on television, that to her Wes was the most interesting man in the world.

"But I'm only twelve," he'd say, like it was part of their routine.

"Okay," she'd say, "the most interesting boy in the world."

She turned back to the stove and pushed a spoon through her sauce. Then she turned back to Wes and wiped her hands on the side of an apron that had WORLD'S GREATEST COOK written across the front.

"Tell me a happy story," she said. "I'll pay you."

It was another part of their routine.

"How much?"

"Ten million dollars," she said. This time when she smiled she really seemed to mean it. "And don't worry, I'm good for it."

So Wes told her about what had happened before he and Mr. Correa had gotten to his dad's apartment, what had happened at open gym, playing as well as he did with the big guys, telling her in great detail what the last play had been like.

For a few minutes, just the two of them in the kitchen, they both *were* happy.

Neither one of them was afraid of the world outside.

TWENTY-THREE

WES AND THE HAWKS HAD a solid week of practice. There were no problems between Wes and Dinero at practice. If you just watched them in scrimmages, and didn't know anything about what had happened between them so far, you wouldn't have believed there had ever been any problems between them.

It wasn't as if they'd suddenly turned into Steph Curry and Kevin Durant, though.

They weren't working together like *that*.

But without them talking about it, they were trying to work together, put it that way. As Emmanuel kept telling Wes, he and Dinero were a work in progress.

Now it was Saturday morning, the big court at Annapolis High and they were getting ready to play the Potomac Valley Rockets, and Wes was hoping that he and Dinero—and everybody else— would play like they'd practiced.

"Things were good this week," E said as they were warming up.

"They've been good before, 'fore they turned bad," Wes said. E grinned.

"Someday," he said, "if I'm really, really lucky, I hope to have a positive attitude like that."

"Hope for the best, prepare for the worst," Wes said. "Who said that?"

E laughed. "*You!*" he said.

"Maybe the one who's a work in progress here is me," Wes said.

"Tell me about it," E said. "Sometimes you remind me about something my mom likes to say, about a sunny day looking for a cloud."

"That's not me, swear," Wes said. "I come to every game hoping it's gonna be the best we're ever gonna play."

"Hold that thought," Emmanuel Pike said, and then Coach Saunders was waving them over and telling them it was time to huddle up.

"Now, this isn't directed at any of you," Coach said when they were all around him. "Fact is, it's directed at all of you. But I want the ball to move today like it's never moved before. I don't want to see any ball stoppers out there. Because when that ball does move, we look like the best team in this whole league. When it doesn't? Y'all still look like five guys on the playground who just met each other."

He was slowly turning as he talked, so they all felt as if he were speaking directly to them.

"Understood?" he said.

Nobody said anything until Wes said, "Understood, Coach."

Then he surprised himself by saying in a loud voice to his teammates, "Who *is* the best team in this league?"

"Hawks are!" they all yelled back at him.

The kid Wes was guarding today, and who was guarding him, was named Davon Gundy. The Rockets' point guard, about the same size as Dinero, was named Paul Peters, with hair that was even more blond than Wes's was, nearly white.

But they weren't the players on the Rockets the Hawks were all looking at, because they were looking at the opposing center, Hassan Jones, who had to be the biggest player in the league, already six three even at the age of twelve. Emmanuel had looked him up on Facebook during the week.

Now E whispered to Wes, "Not sure they even measure that guy in feet and inches. More like they do with skyscrapers, and go by floors." E looked around as if he were scared and whispered again to Wes, "I want my mommy."

"Now who's got the bad attitude?" Wes said to him.

"Oh, heck," Emmanuel Pike said, "let's knock him down to size along with the rest of them."

"Sounds like a plan," Wes said.

Forget about preparing for the worst, he thought, now that the game was starting. Forget about everything. Just go make this the best Saturday of the whole season.

Now *that*, he told himself, was a plan.

TWENTY-FOUR

HASSAN JONES, IN ALL WAYS, turned out to be a load. DeAndre Hill couldn't handle him. Neither could Emmanuel, when Coach switched him over. It was why, a minute into the second quarter, Coach called a quick timeout, called them over, and said they were going to try the box-and-one defense they practiced occasionally. One man would still be guarding Hassan. The other four players would go into a two-two zone.

"Who's gonna be the one on Hassan?" Wes asked.

"You are," Coach Saunders said.

He had a big smile on his face, as if he'd just given Wes the best news in the world.

Wes's response was to look over his shoulder, as if Coach Saunders had to be talking to someone behind him, because he couldn't possibly be talking to Wes.

"Wait," Wes said, "you really are talking to me?"

"Yup."

"Coach," Wes said, "you know I don't back down from a challenge. But the guy is, like, twice my size."

Coach said, "Haven't you ever heard the one about how it's not the size of the dog in the fight, it's the size of the fight in the dog?"

"No," Wes said.

"Well, now you have. You're my best on-the-ball defender," Coach said. "I want you to guard like that when he *doesn't* have the ball. And when he does, I'll get you help."

The Hawks had been trailing by eight points when Coach made the switch on defense and put Wes on Hassan. But with two minutes left in the half, they were ahead by six. The box-and-one was working. Wes sometimes did feel as if he were playing in the shadow of a tall building. But the longer the second quarter wore on, he and the rest of the Hawks could see their new defense wearing on Hassan Jones.

It wasn't just defense. The Hawks started to pick it up on offense. The ball still wasn't moving as much as Wes thought it should and Coach said he wanted it to. But Dinero wasn't as bad as he'd been the game before. He wasn't shooting as much, and he seemed to have remembered the kind of passer he could be.

Better yet, he started to feature Wes as they were making their run, hitting him on the break a couple of times, throwing him the ball as soon as he got open, even signaling for a couple of isolation plays so Wes could post up Davon. Wes didn't know how many points he had. He was never that guy. But he was getting his today.

By the half, the Hawks were ahead by ten points. But as well as Wes had played, at both ends of the court, he felt as if he'd played a whole game already. That was how much of a grind it had been going up against Hassan Jones.

At halftime, he sat next to Emmanuel at the end of the bench and went through one bottle of water and immediately reached for another.

E poked him with an elbow.

"Remember what Coach said about the fight in the dog?" he said. "Dude, you look dog-tired."

"Nah," Wes said. "I'm good. And we're winning. All that matters."

"You know Coach is gonna stick with this defense, right?" E said. "You got another half in you to mix it up with the big guy?"

"You know I do," Wes said. "After we win the game, I'll just go lie on your couch and have you get me things."

"Sure you're not tired?"

"Just of you asking me if I'm tired!" Wes said.

He stayed on Hassan. The Rockets finally figured out that there was no point in forcing the ball into him the way the box-and-one was tying him up in knots. Even that didn't work. The Hawks stretched their lead out to fourteen points. Life was good.

Until the bad Dinero suddenly showed up in the gym.

And decided it was time for him to be the show.

If it were football, Wes thought, the announcers would have talked about him going into his touchdown dance before he crossed the goal line. He started to make the fancy pass instead of the easy one. He forced drives and shots when he should have been doing what he was doing in the first half, and kicking the ball off to Wes, or inside to E or DeAndre when they were open down low.

Coach took him out and replaced him with Josh Amaro, even though Dinero didn't like it. But by the time he did, the momentum of the game had changed, that fast. The Rockets continued to cut into the Hawks' lead, which was down to ten. Then six. Coach put Dinero back in to start the fourth quarter. Didn't change anything, now that the game had changed. Things were going the Rockets' way now, even though they were still behind. Sometimes the scoreboard was wrong, Wes knew. Sometimes you were losing even when the scoreboard said you were still ahead. That's what was happening now in the gym at Annapolis High School. Wes knew, being out there. He just knew. It was as if everybody were suddenly breathing different air.

Coach got Dinero out of there again after the Rockets tied the game. The Hawks briefly started to match them basket for basket, but then Josh fell hard when he was fouled going to the basket. He popped back up, knocked down a couple of free throws. But Coach didn't like the way he was moving, and signaled for Dinero to get back in there.

All Coach said as Dinero passed him was, "Five-man game, from here to the end. Got it?" He stepped pretty hard on his question, and Dinero knew enough to just nod and say, "Got it."

We'll see, Wes thought.

Now they were all in a fight. Davon put the Rockets up by a basket with two minutes left on a neat drive. Wes came over and cut him off, but Davon switched to his left hand, his off hand, and made the shot anyway. But he was slow getting back on defense.

Wes busted it up the court, got himself into space. He maybe could have driven himself. Instead, he pulled up and drained a three.

Hawks by one.

He didn't make that money motion Dinero liked to make with his fingers. He could have, though. He knew the shot was money as soon as he released it.

It was 45–44.

They were still in the box-and-one. But now Dinero was slow getting out on Davon, and Davon was the one who made a long three.

Rockets, 47–45.

Fifty seconds left.

Hawks' ball.

Dinero passed the ball to Wes on the right. Davon ran at him, because it was the same spot from which Wes had just made the three. Only this time Wes didn't have as much room. So he up-faked Davon, drove around him, pulled up before Hassan could get out on him, made a ten-footer.

Game tied at 47.

It was all money now, Wes thought. He was going to miss a shot eventually.

Just not today.

At the other end, Dinero and Russ Adams doubled Davon, who had been feeling it himself the past few minutes. Bottled up, Davon made the right play and threw it inside to Hassan. But Hassan made the mistake that even the best big guys made sometimes when they had a smaller man guarding them:

He brought the ball down before he tried to wheel into his move to the basket.

And now he and Wes were the same size.

Wes was ready for him as soon as the ball came down, reached in for it, stripped Hassan cleanly, made the steal. Gave a quick look at the clock at the other end of the court, behind the Hawks' basket.

Fifteen seconds left.

He outletted the ball over to Dinero. Dinero pushed. As Wes crossed half-court, he made eye contact with Emmanuel. And E knew what Wes wanted the way he knew his phone number.

He came running up, set a perfect screen on Davon, as clean as Wes's steal had just been. Russ was already in the right corner. No worries. Wes ran to the opposite corner.

Wide open.

All Dinero needed to do was pass him the ball one more time.

He didn't.

Instead he put his head down, got a step on Paul, pulled up at the free-throw line even though he hadn't attempted a jumper that Wes remembered the whole fourth quarter, and released his shot with five seconds left.

He shot it too hard, the ball bouncing off the back rim, falling to the left side of the basket.

It looked like they were going to overtime.

To everybody except Wes Davies.

He hadn't stopped to watch Dinero's shot the way everybody else on the court had. He was following the ball and the play all the way, moving toward the basket from the left corner as soon as Dinero released the ball, just the way he had been taught.

Nobody boxed him out. Nobody slowed him down. It was

why, one last time today, it was his ball, not Dinero's or anybody else's.

He didn't have to wait for anybody to pass it this time.

Wes went and got it himself.

He felt the ball come down into his hands as he was going up, putting his soft touch on the putback, the ball hitting perfectly off the backboard and falling softly through the net.

He heard three things in the gym at Annapolis High, one after another.

Wes heard the horn sound, meaning the game was over and the Hawks had won.

He heard the cheer from the section of the stands where the Hawks' parents, including Wes's mom, were sitting.

And then he heard a man's voice from the other side of the court, the man yelling his head off.

"Hey! *Throw my boy the damn ball!*"

Wes knew without looking who that voice belonged to.

In that moment, in front of everybody, it was like Lt. Michael Davies had turned into Lonzo Ball's dad, which meant the worst and loudest basketball dad in the world.

TWENTY-FIVE

WES JUST WATCHED IT HAPPEN, unable to do anything to stop it, frozen in place.

After all the noise at the end of the game, the gym had gotten as quiet as his mom's library at Annapolis High.

His dad's familiar Orioles cap was on his head, just not straight, slightly to the side. He was wearing one of his favorite red flannel shirts, hanging outside his jeans.

He looked unsteady as he made his way to the court.

"Boy was hot as a pistol down the stretch!" he yelled. "You don't make him *work* to get the damn ball! You just give him the rock and let him win the game!"

Wes knew he was really talking about—or talking to—Dinero Rey. Wes looked for him, found him standing in front of the Hawks' bench, eyes big.

His dad was in the middle of the court by now. For some reason he had a ball cocked on his hip.

Wes thought that if his dad had been drinking when he'd come to the house last weekend, he had been drinking a lot more before he came to the game today.

But at the house, only Wes and his mom had seen.

Now everybody could see.

And hear.

"You got to feed the hot hand in this game!"

He put out his right arm, kept the ball on his hip with his left.

"Am I right?" he yelled.

Then Michael Davies saw where Wes was standing and waved at him.

Wes couldn't move.

There was a part of him that wanted to help him, get him out of here. But a much bigger part of him wanted to run the other way.

Fortunately, his mom had made her way down to the court now, too. At the same moment, Coach Saunders took a couple of tentative steps in the direction of Wes's dad.

But Wes, forcing himself to move, beat them both.

"Dad," he said in a voice as quiet as his dad's had been loud, "please stop."

He put a hand on his dad's right arm.

But Michael Davies yanked it away.

"What are you talking about?" he said. "I'm your father!"

"Not like this you're not," Christine Davies said. She placed her arm around Wes.

Wes's dad lowered his eyes and his voice in the same moment.

"I was trying to help out my boy," he said in a voice that you could have scraped off the court in that moment.

"I think," Wes's mom said, "you've helped him enough for one day."

With that, Wes's dad turned and started walking toward the double doors that led to the lobby of the gym, and then the parking lot beyond. He banged slightly into one of the doors, somehow hanging on to his ball, as he disappeared.

He had told everybody that he was trying to help his son.

But who was going to help him?

TWENTY-SIX

FOR SOME REASON, WES LOOKED up at the scoreboard once his dad was gone, even though Wes could still hear his voice, as if it were echoing all around the gym.

The final score was still up there. The clock read 00:00. But he wanted to turn back that clock somehow, just a couple of seconds. A couple of ticks. He wanted it to be the part of Saturday right before the game was about to end right. When everything still felt right. He wanted to go back to the way he felt when he was blowing past everybody on the baseline to get that offensive rebound, and then when the ball was leaving his fingertips and he knew—he just flat knew—that his shot was going in and that the Hawks were going to win the game.

He was still staring at the scoreboard when he felt a hand on his shoulder. He knew it wasn't his mom. Somehow, being his mom, she'd known that he didn't want her to stay out on the court with him, like she was protecting him somehow. So she had gone back to stand with E's parents and give him room.

It was Coach Saunders.

"You okay?" he said.

"Not so much."

Coach was a big man, bigger than Hassan Jones, six four at least. Wes thought he looked a lot like the actor Denzel Washington, who'd been in one of his all-time favorite old movies, one he'd watched over and over again with his dad, *Remember the Titans*. He never talked much about his own basketball career, but Wes had looked him up and knew that he'd been a pretty good baller in his day at Loyola, in Baltimore, a tough small forward who could shoot and rebound.

"You go be with our team now," Coach said, leaning down so only Wes could hear what he was saying, almost like he was telling Wes a secret. "Time like this is what a team is for." Coach paused. "But if you want to talk about this later, you call me, hear?"

"I'm not much of a talker," Wes said.

He turned and looked up and saw Coach smile. "Kind of picked up on that by now," he said to Wes.

"Nothing much *to* talk about," Wes said. "Everybody here saw."

"I just want you to know that I'm here for you," Coach said. "We all are."

Wes thanked him. They walked together toward the bench. Wes's mom was behind the bench, talking to E's mom and dad, but keeping her eyes on Wes. Josh's mother had brought the snacks today, cookies and Gatorade and bananas and apples and water bottles and juice bottles. Mrs. Amaro, they all knew, did it up right as their team mom.

Wes sat down in the middle of the bench, teammates on both sides of him. Them being there with him, as if they were establishing some kind of perimeter, didn't make what had happened a few minutes ago go away. Nobody could make what had just happened go away, not now and maybe not ever.

But Wes, the team guy, somehow felt better having his team around him this way, as Josh and Russ and E started to replay the last few minutes of the game, going over it, possession by possession, until they got to the Hawks' last possession, and how the only one of them who really kept playing until the horn sounded, the way Coach told them to, was Wes.

He'd been the one to go get the ball when no one else did.

"Player making a play, is all that was," E said, as if he were broadcasting his statement to everybody still left in the gym.

Even Dinero chimed in. "We went from a low-percentage shot, which happened to be mine, to a high-percentage shot." He pointed at Wes. "Yours," Dinero said.

"Thanks," Wes said. "But anybody could have done it. Nobody put a body on me. It was like I was chasing down one of my own misses in my driveway."

"Anybody *could* have done it," DeAndre said. "But you *did*."

"Should have seen the look on Hassan's face," E said. "He was, like, where'd that boy with the Porzingis hair come from?"

They all laughed as Wes self-consciously ran a hand through his hair. He *did* wear it a little bit like Kristaps Porzingis of the Knicks. They pretty much had the same light hair color and the last time Wes had gotten his hair cut, he'd actually printed a picture of Porzingis to show the barber, telling him that's the way he wanted it, shaved close on the sides and with what E called a fade in front.

"Got lucky," Wes said.

"Got us a game, is what you did," Russ Adams said.

Finally it was time for them to all leave. Wes's mom was over talking to Coach Saunders, but whatever she was saying to him couldn't have been too grim, because he was smiling and nodding. E asked Wes if he still wanted to hang out later. Wes said he'd call after he got home.

Wes went to his bag, took out his shooting shirt, put it back on, started to walk out to where his mom and Coach were standing at midcourt. Where his dad had been.

As Wes did, he realized that Dinero was walking with him.

"Hey," Dinero said.

"Hey," Wes said.

"That was bad," he said. "With your dad. Even though I know I'm not telling you anything you don't know."

"He's been like that before," Wes said. "Just not in public."

"Just wanted to say I feel for you. Can't be easy dealing with that, him going all LaVar Ball on you."

"Yeah," Wes said. He wondered how Lonzo Ball had dealt with his dad when he was growing up.

"You must be really mad at him," Dinero said.

That made Wes pause. "Not really."

Dinero stopped. So did Wes. They turned to face each other.

"You're not mad at him?" Dinero said. "For real?"

"I feel bad for him, not mad," Wes said.

"After what he just did to you?" Dinero said. "No way."

Wes shook his head. "It's more like something he did to himself because he couldn't help himself," Wes said. "He doesn't want to be the way he is right now. Whatever happened to him in the war, he didn't want any of that stuff. He probably didn't want today to happen. But like I said, he just can't help himself."

Dinero blew out some air and said, "Wow, you really mean that, don't you?"

"I really mean it," Wes said.

"So what are you going to do?" Dinero said.

"Find him," Wes said.

"If you do, what are you going to say to him?" Dinero asked.

"Maybe thank him."

Dinero shook his head, as if he might not have heard right.

"*Thank* him?" he said to Wes. "For what?"

"For being here." He nodded and said, "At least he was here."

TWENTY-SEVEN

"**D**O YOU THINK HE'S HAD time to walk there?" Wes's mom asked.

Wes said that there had been more than enough time since the game ended.

Then Wes said, "And he wouldn't have tried to drive, right?"

"Even in an impaired state," Christine Davies said, "I don't believe your father would ever put someone else in harm's way. I may have trouble recognizing who your father is these days, but I still know him better than anyone."

She gave a quick sidelong glance at Wes when they came to a stop sign.

"Why do you think he's there?" she asked.

"Because he had that old ball with him," Wes said.

"And you think he'll be willing to talk to you?"

"Maybe not," Wes said. "But he won't be able to hide the way he did when I went to his apartment."

He told his mom what he'd told Dinero: as badly as his dad had behaved today, at least he had been there.

They were on their way to a small park a couple of blocks away from the rec center, with a basketball court—a half-court, really—that hardly anybody used anymore for pickup games, because the outdoor courts at the rec center were so good. His dad used to take Wes there after dinner occasionally, saying that they had to get out of the driveway and let his game breathe. The surface of the court needed work, and Michael Davies kept replacing the nets himself when they were torn or simply gone. Hardly anybody ever played there, especially in the early evening.

Wes's dad called it their secret basketball place.

There were no lights, even though they could see the lights from the court at the rec center and hear games going on over there. But they'd work on things until it got too dark, and sometimes even after that. Just the two of them.

When his dad had gotten back from Afghanistan this time, he'd go over there alone sometimes, not asking Wes if he wanted to go with him, as if now he'd needed a secret basketball place all his own.

Wes asked his mom to stop the car at the entrance to the park, where the kids' playground was. He said he probably wouldn't be long. She said that if his dad was there to take as much time as he needed.

He walked across the playground and heard the bounce of a basketball, a pause, and then heard the sound of the ball banging off the rim.

He saw his dad, alone out there.

He looked the same as he had at the game, except that he'd stuffed the Orioles cap into the back pocket of his jeans, which seemed to be hanging on him even more than they had when he'd come to the house, as if he'd lost more weight in the past week. He didn't seem unsteady, at least not here, the way he had at the gym. He just looked slow as he chased down a missed shot, so much slower than Wes remembered him being when they used to come here together.

Now they were together here again.

But not anything like the way they used to be.

Wes still didn't announce himself. He just watched as his dad dribbled toward the faded free-throw line, measured his shot, squared himself up, and put up a set shot that was too short, and barely clipped the front of the rim on the way down. There was, Wes noticed, no net.

As he walked after the ball—he'd always make Wes run after missed shots—Wes said, "You call that a follow-through?"

His dad didn't turn right away. Wes saw his shoulders slump, as if he'd been caught, like a kid doing something wrong. He reached down and picked up the ball and was already shaking his head, even that move slow, as he did finally turn in Wes's direction.

"You shouldn't have followed me here," Michael Davies said.

"I didn't actually follow you, Dad," Wes said. "I sort of figured it out."

"Same thing."

"I wanted to talk," Wes said.

"You might want to talk about it," his dad said, "but I don't."

"Okay," Wes said. "Maybe I'll just shoot around with you a little bit."

He hadn't changed out of his game sneakers. But he didn't care. He wasn't even sure what he thought was going to happen now.

He took a couple of steps out onto the court.

His dad shook his head, more vigorously than before.

"You need to go," he said.

Then: "Where's your mother?"

"Waiting in the car."

"She knew I wouldn't want to talk to her, either," his dad said.

"You always said she was the smartest one of all of us," Wes said.

"At least that hasn't changed, even if everything else has," he said.

They stood there looking at each other. The ball was back on his dad's hip, the way it had been at Annapolis High. More than anything in that moment, Wes was hoping his dad would pass him the ball.

But he didn't.

It was like the weirdest playground stare-down that Wes Davies had ever been in, like they were each waiting for the other to make the first move.

Finally his dad said, "I'm sorry."

Wes realized how much he didn't want to hear those words. He wanted his dad to be tough. He wanted his old dad back. "You don't have to apologize," Wes said.

"Yeah," his dad said. "Yeah, I do. Sometimes you gotta man up when you let people down."

Suddenly he took the ball off his hip and got it into both hands and raised it over his head and then slammed it down in front of him before managing to catch it.

"I'm sorry for everything," Michael Davies said.

He made no move to come closer. Neither did Wes.

Wes said, "You were there the other day, weren't you? At your apartment when I went over there?"

His dad nodded.

"Why didn't you come to the door?" Wes said.

"I was embarrassed," he said. "Your mom was right to call me out like she did and I knew it. I was ashamed and didn't want to see anybody."

"I'm not just anybody," Wes said. And just like that, no warning, he felt himself wanting to cry. But he wasn't going to let it happen.

His dad said, "You were such a good player today."

Wes couldn't tell whether he was saying it with pride in his voice or hurt. Or both.

And he couldn't hold in the question he'd been wanting to ask anymore.

"Dad," he said, "please tell me what happened to you. What made you like this?"

Another quick shake of the head from him.

"I gotta go," he said.

Wes was the one shouting now.

"Why won't you just tell us?" he said. "Why won't you let us help you? *Please let us help you.*"

"Wes . . . I really gotta go."

"At least let Mom drive you."

"Rather walk," he said. "You know what they say about guys in the condition I was in today. Air will do me good."

Finally he threw Wes a bounce pass. Wes caught it and threw him a bounce pass right back.

"You're still a great teammate, kid," his dad said.

Then he turned and walked in the other direction, away from the playground and away from the street where Wes's mom had parked the car.

It wasn't until Wes was back inside the car that he remembered he hadn't gotten the chance to thank his dad for coming to the game.

TWENTY-EIGHT

THE HAWKS KEPT WINNING. WES'S dad stayed away. That was the story of the next few weeks of his life, as the season moved into January.

And Dinero was still Dinero.

As talented as he was, it was still as if he couldn't get out of his own way sometimes, even with the Hawks going good, even looking like the best team in the league.

He would be going along and looking every bit as much a team guy as Wes was, or Emmanuel Pike, who couldn't have been more unselfish on the court if he tried. He would go long stretches of games and be a pass-first point guard, and totally play the game the right way.

Then, all of a sudden, without warning, he'd turn back into the Money Man. The hey-look-at-me Dinero who attempted hot-dog passes and acrobatic drives to the basket almost for the fun of it. The thing of it was, he would make them work a lot of the time, which made it hard to be mad at him. Wes even found himself admiring some of the things Dinero could do on the court. That line between playing selfishly and unselfishly wasn't always so clear when he was scoring buckets and the Hawks were winning games by ten points or more. Sure, Wes and the other guys were getting fewer touches, but was that a bad thing? Wes knew his dad would think so.

One person who definitely thought so was Coach, who would sit Dinero down for a few minutes whenever Coach thought he was out of control. Wes would look over at them when there'd be a break in the action in the game and see Coach talking and Dinero nodding, neither one of them seemingly paying attention to what the rest of the Hawks were doing.

When Dinero would get back out there, he'd play as if he'd learned whatever lessons Coach had been teaching him on the bench, and sometimes things would be fine for the rest of the game.

Wes remembered something he'd read about Magic Johnson, how it was as if there were two of him: Magic and Earvin, which was his real first name. Earvin Johnson, they used to say when he was still playing, was the perfect teammate with the perfect basketball values, always looking to make the right pass, set up the right shot, either for himself or his Laker teammates. But then when the Showtime Lakers would get rolling, it was Magic who took over, doing fancy things on the court almost like he wanted to play for the Harlem Globetrotters.

Even at twelve, Wes could see some of that in Dinero, as if he couldn't help himself, even when he'd find himself getting the kind of timeout from Coach your parents used to give you when you were little and had misbehaved. Wes wondered what Dinero's dad thought about the way he acted on the court. But when Wes would find him in the stands, he'd just be sitting there in the same pose, arms folded in front of him. Mr. Rey showed no emotion about what Dinero or anybody else was doing out there. It was like Mr. Rey thought of basketball as a business and Dinero was just doing his work.

In Wes's mind, Dinero had gotten better at keeping his ego under control as the season went along. And things seemed to have gotten better between them, certainly since the Rockets' game, that day Wes's dad had come out onto the court.

Wes hadn't seen his dad since that day at the park. As far as Wes knew, he hadn't snuck into any of his games. His mom said she'd called him a few times, just to check in, but he wasn't answering his phone or returning her calls.

"Do you think he might have left Annapolis without telling us?" Wes said one night at dinner.

"No. He's been seeing a therapist at the Naval Academy once a week," Wes's mom said. "A friend of mine who's a nurse has seen him there."

"You could go over there and try to talk to him," Wes said.

She shook her head. "Therapy is an intensely private thing," she said, "especially for a private man like your father."

"At least he's making an effort to get help," Wes said. "That counts for something."

"It counts for a lot. There's a part of him that understands he can't do this alone," she said. "So, there's that. There's just no room for us, at least not now."

All along Wes had thought that somehow basketball would bring him back. He'd clung to that. Now he wondered. Maybe the way his dad had embarrassed himself and embarrassed Wes that day drove him away from this season, maybe for good. So, Wes had lost him, at least for now, even as the Hawks kept winning.

Maybe their most impressive win yet was the one they'd had today, on the road against the Northern Virginia Spurs. The Spurs had been undefeated before today. But the Hawks jumped on them early and led by sixteen points at the half.

But then the Spurs showed why they had the record they did. It was a combination of things. Their shooters started to make the shots they'd been missing in the first half. And the Hawks started missing the shots they'd been making.

Dinero wasn't helping matters very much by trying to do too much himself. His shooting had gone cold but he kept forcing difficult shots when Wes or Emmanuel were open—if not for their own shot then at least for a pass. It was like the more Dinero missed, the more stubborn he grew.

This time when Coach Saunders put him on the bench, halfway through the second half, he decided to keep him there. Josh, who normally would have replaced Dinero at point guard, had four fouls, so Coach moved Wes to the point, where he proceeded to take over the game without taking a single shot.

The funny thing was, Wes had been having a good shooting day up until then. The Spurs had seen this, and with Dinero out of the game, they figured Wes would be the Hawks' first option on offense. As soon as he brought the ball up the court, the Spurs' defense began keying on him. So he did what any good point guard would do: He passed to the open man.

First Russ hit a couple of shots. Then Emmanuel and DeAndre started playing a nifty two-man game in the low blocks. No matter who it was, there was always someone open for a shot, so Wes kept feeding them. E ended up in double figures for the first time all season, and it was the also the first time that Russ ended up feeling like part of the offense. Wes loved it, knowing that it would build their confidence and make the team stronger.

"First place is gonna be ours," E said when the game was over. "Slam dunk."

Wes shook his head.

"No slam dunks in basketball," he said. "Not when you're our age."

It was the middle of the afternoon when the doorbell rang. For some reason, and even though he hadn't seen his dad in weeks, Wes thought it might be him. Maybe his dad had been hiding somewhere in the gym in Alexandria. Maybe he'd seen with his own eyes the way Wes had played down the stretch and the way the Hawks had looked.

Maybe his dad wanted to surprise him.

There was a surprise waiting for him when he opened the front door, only not the one Wes was hoping for or one he expected.

"Can I come in?" Dinero Rey asked.

TWENTY-NINE

WES DIDN'T KNOW WHAT TO say at first.

"Who's there?" he heard his mom say from behind him.

Wes stepped aside so she could see Dinero.

"Well, Dinero, this is a surprise," she said.

You're telling me, Wes thought.

"Wesley Davies," his mom said, "are you just going to stand there like a statue or are you going to invite the young man in while I go check on my cookies?"

"Sorry," Wes said to Dinero. "I just wasn't expecting to see you here."

Dinero gave Wes one of his best smiles.

"Guess what?" he said. "Neither was I."

They were still standing there in the doorway.

"I didn't even know you knew where I live," Wes said.

"Coach gave me the address," Dinero said.

"How'd you get here?" Wes said. He was looking past him, and didn't see a car on the street.

"My dad drove me," Dinero said, "and said he'd be back for me later."

"Come on in," Wes said.

Dinero followed him into the house. Wes wasn't sure where to take him, into the living room or the kitchen, or upstairs to his room or outside to the driveway.

What the heck was he doing here?

His mom saved him, at least for the time being.

"Why don't you two come back here to the kitchen?" she called out to them. "My killer chocolate chip cookies are going to be ready to be devoured by hungry young men in about two minutes."

Dinero followed Wes back to the kitchen. His mom already had a plate of chocolate chip cookies on the table that looked big enough to feed the entire Hawks team. She told Dinero that Wes usually had milk with the cookies when they were fresh out of the oven. Dinero said milk would be fine.

They sat across from each other and didn't really have to start up a conversation because they were too busy eating. After a few minutes Dinero smiled at Wes's mom and said these were the best chocolate chip cookies he'd ever had in his life, but she had to swear not to tell his own mom that he'd said that. Christine Davies smiled back at him and said that his secret was most assuredly safe with her.

"Another win for the Hawks today," Wes's mom said.

"Thanks to Number Thirteen," Dinero said. "I got to watch same as you did, Mrs. Davies."

"Could just as easily have been you out there at the end passing the ball around," Wes said.

Dinero even managed to smile about that.

"Coach might disagree," Dinero said.

"Hey, all that matters is that we won," Wes said. "I pretended I was you when I started to get a few assists."

"More than a few," Dinero said.

Somehow, even in his own kitchen, Wes couldn't stop himself from being a team player. Maybe his dad was right. Maybe being that kind of team guy really was in his DNA. It was something else Wes had learned once from his dad: About DNA. And not just as your makeup applied to basketball.

"Sometimes my ego gets in the way of my own game," Dinero said now.

"Happens to everybody," Wes said, "all the way from seventh grade to the NBA."

They went back to eating cookies until Wes's mom said, "Listen, you two seventh-grade basketball stars. I've got bills to pay upstairs. If you want more cookies, they're in the cookie jar next to the fridge."

"Mom," Wes said, "if I eat any more cookies, Dinero will have to roll me like a basketball out to the driveway after."

"Speak for yourself," Dinero said. "My dad likes to say that the two most beautiful words in the world are 'more pie.' With me, it's 'more cookies.'"

Wes's mom left. Now it was just the two of them in the kitchen. It occurred to Wes that he was feeling more pressure to make conversation—with one of his teammates—than he did when he was at the free-throw line in a close game.

Or driving to the basket.

And sometimes, he thought, the easier way to get there was in a straight line.

"Why are you here?" he said to Dinero.

The way he just came out with it made Dinero laugh.

"It's not a short answer," he said.

"You got somewhere to be besides here?" Wes said.

Dinero shook his head.

"Me neither," Wes said. "There's no shot clock in my mom's kitchen. Take as much time as you need."

Whatever needed to be worked out between them, maybe they could work it out once and for all.

Dinero said he'd been wanting to come over and talk to Wes like this since Wes's dad had come out of the stands after the Rockets' game, and Wes had told Dinero he was going after him.

"Some of the guys told me after about how he just got back from being in the army, right?" Dinero said.

"Navy," Wes said. "A Navy SEAL."

"Like the ones we studied in history?" Dinero said. "Like the guys who tracked down and killed Osama bin Laden?"

"Like that," Wes said. "He was in Afghanistan."

They weren't talking about whatever reason had brought Dinero here today. But it was all right. They were here and they were talking, and that wasn't nothing, as E liked to say.

"SEALs are like the best of the best, right?" Dinero said.

"Like a whole unit of navy LeBrons," Wes said.

"Like a Dream Team," Dinero said.

Well, yeah, Wes thought, until you feel like one of their lives has turned into a nightmare.

"I'm still sorry for what happened that day," Dinero said.

"You didn't do anything," Wes said.

"No, see, that's the thing," Dinero said, leaning forward. "I'm not apologizing about what your dad did. I'm apologizing for what I did."

"Not sure I understand," Wes said. "You didn't do anything."

"Actually I did," Dinero said. "Because everybody in the gym knew he was really yelling about me that day."

Wes started to say something, was about to tell him that he'd moved on from the way that game ended, just like he'd moved on from what his dad had done. But Dinero put a hand up to stop him, almost like he'd anticipated a move Wes was about to make.

"Don't even bother denying it," Dinero said. "You know it was true. He was mad at me because I didn't pass you the ball."

"We won," Wes said. "It's all that matters, like I said before."

"But it does matter," Dinero said. "I've been thinking about that ever since, too. Because think about it: If I'd passed you the ball like I should have and you'd knocked down one more jumper, he would never have started yelling or come out on the court or any of that."

"You don't know that," Wes said. "Maybe something else would have gotten him going. My mom says people hardly ever know what they're going to do when they've had too much to drink."

Wes really didn't know what to say now.

"It took me a while to screw up my courage and come over here," Dinero said. "Probably surprises you, since I know how cocky everybody thinks I am. But what happened to you that day is really on *me*."

Wes sat there. From next door he heard the neighbors' dog barking. From upstairs he heard his mom talking to somebody on the telephone.

"How about I say, apology accepted, and we just go from there?" Wes said.

Dinero shook his head.

"It's not everything I came here to say today," he said. "What I really came here to do is ask you to help me."

"Help you with what?" Wes said.

"Help me be more like you in basketball," Dinero Rey said.

"Get out of here," Wes said. "You're already great at basketball. You're the best player I've ever played with, pretty much."

Dinero nodded.

"I've always been the best player on every team I've ever played *on*," Dinero said.

It didn't come out in a cocky way, just like he was stating a fact.

"But that's why I've never had to be a great teammate," Dinero continued. "Do you get what I'm trying to tell you? Everybody else always had to be a good teammate to me, and that's why I never had to learn to be one myself."

"It's not like a class you can take," Wes said. "I can't teach somebody how to do that."

"I think you can," Dinero said.

"It was my dad who taught me," Wes said.

"See, that's the thing!" Dinero said. He slapped the table so hard it made their glasses and the plate between them jump a little. "Your dad taught you that it's all about the team. From the time I got good at basketball, my dad has been saying it all has to be about *me*. He's the one like Lonzo Ball's dad, except the only one who hears it from him *is* me."

Dinero smiled. "I was doing what my dad taught me that day against the Rockets," he said. "And your dad got mad because I wasn't being like you."

Without another word he stood up and took their glasses over to the sink and cleaned them, and put them on the counter. Then he came back and took the cookie plate and did the same thing.

"Let's go," Dinero said then.

"Where?"

"That basket I saw in your driveway?" he said. "That's the same one I have at home. Let's go play some ball."

Wes grinned.

"My basket, my ball, my rules," he said.

"I feel you," Dinero said.

Wes said, "About time!"

This time they both laughed.

Wes told Dinero where the ball was. He ran upstairs to get his sneakers since he'd been walking around in flip-flops when Dinero had shown up.

His mom was waiting for him at the top of the stairs.

"I might have overheard a little of what you two were talking about," she said.

"Mom!" Wes said, trying to act outraged, both of them knowing he wasn't. "You were spying on us?"

She put a finger to her lips. "Shh," she said. "I don't want Dinero to hear that I heard."

"Sorry," he said.

"And by the way?" she said. "You may call it spying. I call it taking a healthy interest in my son's life."

"Fine, have it your way," he said.

"As much as you guys play like men sometimes, and as much as you have both looked up to the men in your lives, you need to remember something," she said. "You're still just boys."

"Your point being?" Wes said.

"Just go outside and be boys," she said. "That's my point."

THIRTY

FOR A LITTLE WHILE IN the driveway, they didn't talk about their dads.

They were just boys.

They didn't play one-on-one today. Wes admitted that he'd never liked playing one-on-one, mostly because he didn't think you learned a whole lot about basketball if what you were doing didn't involve passing the ball.

"I know you still have to play with your head up in one-on-one," Wes said to Dinero. "But somehow when I'm doing it, I feel like I'm playing with my head *down*."

"Never thought of it that way," Dinero said. "So maybe I've already learned something today."

"I don't learn anything when it's just me against somebody else," Wes said. "Going up against each other we're not learning how to play *with* each other."

Dinero shook his head. "My dad kept telling me that I had to watch out for you," he said.

"Guess what?" Wes said. "My dad told me the same thing about you."

"Yeah," Dinero said, "and then I made him look like a genius when I wouldn't pass you the ball."

Dinero had the ball. He spun away from Wes with a lightning move Wes had seen him use in games. He started to pull up for a jumper. But Wes had a feeling he wasn't shooting, so he cut to the basket. Dinero finished his shooting motion with an empty right hand, because he was shoveling a perfect underhand pass to Wes with his left.

Then Wes caught the ball with his left hand, and in one motion, already in midair, he scooped the ball off the backboard.

"Hey," Dinero said, "we should try that in a game one of these days."

"If we do, I better make the shot," Wes said, "or we'll both be sitting next to Coach."

"He can sit one of us down and win, we already proved that," Dinero said. "But not both of us."

Making it sound like they were a team, within their team. Or as if they were introducing themselves to each other all over again, closer to the end of the season than the beginning.

Wes knew it wasn't as if all of their problems were going to disappear in one afternoon. But maybe they were both learning today, mostly about each other. Mostly they were passing each other the ball, from all parts of the driveway and all angles. They invented plays, imagining where imaginary screeners and imaginary defenders were. They came up with a drill that no matter where either of them was on the driveway court—even if they weren't facing each other—as soon as one guy yelled, "Open," a clean pass had to be made in that moment. The more they did it, the better they got at it, as if they could find each other with their eyes closed.

"I got another one," Dinero said. "No matter which one of us has the ball, if the other thinks he can get open on a cut, all he has to do is this."

He made his money motion with his fingers.

"Seriously?" Wes said.

"Might as well finally make the move useful," Dinero Rey said.

"I've never done that before in my life," Wes said.

"First time for everything," Dinero said.

They bumped fists. And kept playing, having lost track of time. Not going against each other. Playing basketball with each other. Wes's mom came to the side door finally and asked if Dinero would like to stay for dinner. He said that he needed to call his parents, but was pretty sure it would be okay with them. Then Wes asked if he could invite Emmanuel over, too. She said to have at it. He went inside and called E, while Dinero was getting out his own phone and calling home.

"You want to come over and shoot around and then have dinner later?" Wes asked Emmanuel.

He heard E ask his mom and heard her in the background telling him that if she was going to give him a ride, it had to be right now, she had some errands to run.

"Be there soon," E said, "as you probably heard."

"Pretty sure I could have heard her without a phone," Wes said. "Get over here, dude. Dinero and I will be waiting for you."

He was waiting to drop that one on him.

"Ex*cuse* me?" E said.

"Yeah," Wes said. "He came over and we've been outside working on stuff ever since."

"You and your nemesis, Dinero?" E said. "*That* Dinero?"

"Shut up and get in the car," Wes said.

When he was back outside, Dinero said, "My parents are cool with me staying."

"Cool," Wes said.

It was crazy, if he really thought about it. He'd been hoping all along that his dad might make his season better. And maybe now, because of what he started by walking onto the court that day, he had.

Wes had the ball. Dinero cut to the basket. Wes grinned and held on to the ball.

"Oh, I get it," Dinero said. "It was your turn not to pass me the ball even though I was open."

"Nope," Wes said.

He rubbed his fingers together.

"You didn't give me the sign," he said.

Wes was nearly back to the sidewalk. Dinero went over near the front walk, made the money motion with his fingers. As soon as he took off, Wes snapped off a long, one-bounce pass that caught him right in stride.

When E got there, they ran some of the plays the Hawks did off high screens, then had him popping out to take short jumpers of his own, which he was knocking down the way he had at the end of the game against the Spurs.

"There's gonna be a big moment before this season is over,"

Dinero said to E, "when the defense is going to back off and dare you to make a shot, and you're gonna make it."

"If you say so," Emmanuel said.

"We *know* so," Wes said.

They stayed out there until Wes's mom called them for dinner. The day got colder, Wes's mom saying it was in the forties. Wes and Dinero and E all wore hoodies, and worked up such a good sweat they didn't care. They ate dinner and had more chocolate chip cookies. Wes's mom put the lights on over the basket, and they went back outside and played until it was time for Dinero and E to leave.

Wes was getting ready for bed when he heard his phone buzzing. He went and picked it up. The screen read, "Unknown Caller." Wes felt his heart beating a little faster because the only unknown caller who ever called him was his dad.

"Hello," he said, hearing the excitement in his own voice.

There was no response. But he could hear people talking in the background and music playing.

"Hello," he said again. "This is Wes. Is that you, Dad?"

There was still no response. Just the voices and the music, until he heard somebody in the background yell, "What does a guy have to do to get a beer around here?"

A bar, Wes thought.

His dad was calling him from a bar.

Had to be.

"Hello," he said one more time.

Nothing except the bar noise. Somebody laughed. There was a cheer. If it was a bar, maybe there was some kind of game on the television.

Wes didn't want it to be a bar, but where else could noise like that be coming from?

He stared at the phone in his hand, put it back to his ear, held it there until the bar noise was gone, and he finally heard the call end. Then Wes turned it off, stuck it in the top drawer of his nightstand, turned off the lights, and got into bed.

The whole day had been money, he thought.

Until it wasn't.

THIRTY-ONE

SOMEHOW THEY WERE STARTING TO close in on the end of the regular season, in first place by themselves now, becoming more certain by the game that they would be one of the teams in their league's Final Four.

Didn't mean it was getting any easier.

Even though things had gotten easier between Wes and Dinero, and even though they both had the best of basketball intentions, they were *still* a work in progress—they were learning to play together all over again.

It reached the point where Coach Saunders had to sit them down and explain that there was such a thing as being too unselfish, as much as he preached unselfishness to them and the rest of the Hawks all the time.

"You guys are so worried about passing the ball, to yourself and everybody else, that you're passing up good shots," Coach said after they'd hung on to beat a really good team from Washington, D.C., the Bulls.

"See," Coach continued, "there always comes the time when the ball is *supposed* to stop. When you're *supposed* to shoot it.

Doesn't matter whether it goes in or not. Not what I'm talking about. It means that the play you just ran—one your old coach drew up for you—actually worked."

Wes knew what he meant. It wasn't that he and Dinero had overpassed in the game they'd just played and won. There were times when they were both so fixed on tracking what the other one was doing that it had nearly cost them a victory. There had been too many times when Wes had the ball and his eyes locked on Dinero the way a quarterback in football only locked in on one receiver. And Dinero had done the same.

They had been tied with the D.C. Bulls at 46 with just over two minutes left to play. Bulls ball. The kid Wes had been guarding for most of the game, Kyle Lester, was shorter than Wes by a couple of inches, but he'd had a solid game. Wes had underestimated him early because of the size advantage he had on him, thinking his length would keep Kyle from shooting over him from the outside. But then he'd found out the hard way—after Kyle knocked down some jumpers—that he had this sneaky way of creating just enough space for himself right before he released the ball.

Now Wes told himself to crowd Kyle even more with the game on the line. As soon as he did, Kyle put the ball on the floor. He seemed to have a step on Wes. But Wes cut him off and forced him to the middle. When he did, Kyle forced up a shot anyway, the kind of shot Dinero kept trying to squeeze off in traffic earlier in the season. The shot hit the front of the rim. Wes, following the play all the way, grabbed the rebound. He heard Coach yell, "Push!" Fine with Wes. He knew they had come from behind in the second half because they had pushed the ball on the break-off after just about every Bulls' miss.

Wes took the ball up the middle himself. Dinero was on his right, E on his left. There were two guys back for the Bulls. Wes ran the three-on-two exactly the way he had always been taught, making the defenders commit themselves first. Making *them* come to *him*. It wasn't much of a coordinated effort. They both tried to pinch on Wes at the same time, leaving both wings open.

As much as E's shot had improved lately, Wes was going to Dinero all the way.

As soon as the ball was in Dinero's hands, Wes thought:

Shoot it.

This time I want you to put it up.

Dinero didn't hesitate.

But he wasn't shooting.

He was passing the ball right back to Wes, almost as if the ball had barely touched his own hands. Wes was so surprised to see the ball coming right back at him that it nearly went through *his* hands. He bobbled it at first, quickly collected it, saw that E was still wide open on the left, and passed the ball to him.

Second option becoming the best option.

E also didn't hesitate. Just pulled up as the defender closest to him slid over, banked home a ten-footer like a champ.

Hawks by two.

At the other end, Kyle Lester made a terrific feed to the Bulls' center and got the kid a layup.

Game tied again.

Under a minute.

The whole season has come down to the last minute, Wes thought.

And, really, who'd want to have it any other way?

The Hawks went right back at them. Dinero had the ball now, near the top of the key. The rest of them spread the court. Wes ran to the right corner. Always his sweet spot. Kyle ran with him. Then they both watched as Dinero just absolutely torched the kid guarding with him with a filthy crossover, leaving the kid frozen in place, taking the ball past the free-throw line and into the middle.

Wes had seen him make this same move in scrimmages plenty of times, breaking down Josh or Russ or even Wes off the dribble this way, having the bigs in front of him at his mercy.

Even when Wes and Dinero weren't getting along, when it really was as if they were playing on opposing teams, it had been fun to watch Dinero operate this way, knowing how many options he had in moments like this.

Like he had the defense defenseless.

So many times, Wes had seen him pull up, even when a big came up on him, and delight in tossing his favorite shot—a teardrop, Dinero called the drop—up and over everybody.

Drop the drop on them now!

It was like Wes was shouting at himself, inside his own brain.

Except at the last moment, as the Bulls' center did get a long arm up, Dinero wheeled and kicked the ball all the way over to Wes, even as covered as Wes was. Kyle nearly beat him to the ball. Didn't.

Wes grabbed it, had time to give a quick check of the shot clock.

Three seconds showing.

Now or never.

He turned—not getting a chance to square himself all the way, almost as if he were shooting sidesaddle—and got the ball airborne even with Kyle right in his face. So Wes was the one forcing a shot now, because he had no choice.

When he let it go, he thought it was too high and too hard.

Maybe a little bit to the right.

But then he watched in amazement as the ball hit high off the backboard and went in.

The Hawks were back up by two.

It was the way the game ended.

It was almost immediately, as soon as they were out of the handshake line, that Coach pulled Wes and Dinero aside, sat them down at the end of the bench, and gave them his speech about unselfishness.

They both did a lot of nodding. They both knew enough about basketball to know that what he was telling them was right. They both said they'd work harder. Coach said that was all he could ask.

"Work harder," he said. "Think better."

But even now Dinero couldn't resist being Dinero.

"But, Coach," he said, "don't they sometimes accuse LeBron of being too unselfish?"

Wes watched Coach grin. It was as if he could see Dinero putting a move on him. But he was ready for it.

"I'm sorry," Coach said, "but are you comparing yourself to LeBron?"

"No, *sir!*" Dinero said.

They were both having fun and knew it.

"But you can appreciate the point your point guard is making," Dinero continued.

"Help me out," Coach said.

"I may be moving the ball too much," he said. "But at least I'm moving it." He smiled. "Just like you keep telling me to."

A big smile from him now, as big as he had. Wes felt himself smiling, too.

Coach turned to Wes and said, "You think this is funny?"

"Fun, Coach," he said. "Just having fun watching the show."

"And would you like to add anything to the conversation?"

Wes said, "We'll both try to be better."

"And smarter," Dinero said.

"More like it," Coach said. Then he looked at both of them, his face suddenly serious, and said, "Not the worst problem in the world to have, even if we needed to get lucky a couple of times there down at the end."

"Fun getting lucky once in a while," Wes said.

"Winning's the most fun," Dinero said, then nodded at Wes and said, "I get that from him, Coach."

Wes went to talk to his mom, and E and E's parents. But as he walked over to them, he could see Dinero's dad waving him over, almost as if he were angry with Dinero, his face red. For most of the season Wes had been waiting for Mr. Rey to show some kind of emotion at these games, to do something more than sit there with his arms crossed.

Finally he was.

Dinero's smile, Wes could see, was already long gone. He

stopped and watched as Dinero and his dad made their way quickly down the sideline, past the Bulls' bench, toward the doors of the rec center. Mr. Rey was doing all the talking. Dinero had his head down as his father clearly gave him an earful, out the door and into the lobby and probably all the way home.

Wes thought:

It's as if Dinero's dad had turned into Lonzo's dad, just without the world hearing everything he had to say.

Or maybe Dinero's dad had been that way all along.

THIRTY-TWO

THERE WAS A MAN SITTING on the front step of the porch when they pulled into the driveway after the game, in the same place Wes's dad had been that time.

For a second, Wes thought it might *be* his dad.

It wasn't.

"Who is that?" Wes said to his mom, before either one of them got out of the car.

"I don't know," she said. "Stay here."

"I'm not afraid to get out of the car, Mom," Wes said.

He saw her smile. "No," she said. "You wouldn't be, would you?"

As they both got out of the car, Christine Davies called out to the man. "Would you mind telling me what you're doing on my front porch?"

The man stood up, smiling, putting his hands up in surrender.

"So sorry, ma'am," he said. "I didn't mean to startle you."

"I don't mean to sound rude," she said. "But who are you?"

"I'm looking for Lieutenant Davies," he said.

"He's not here," she said. "And you still haven't told me who you are."

"My name is Anthony Phillips," he said. "Lieutenant Davies knew me as Chief Petty Officer Phillips."

He came up the sidewalk, and for a second, before he stuck out his hand, Wes thought he might salute.

He was tall and young-looking and had the same kind of short, scruffy beard as Mr. Correa. Wes thought he looked big enough to have been a football player.

"This was the only address I had for him," he said to Wes's mom.

"Why are you looking for him?" she said.

The young guy said, "I wanted to thank him for something."

"Thank him for what, if you don't mind me asking?" Christine Davies said.

"For saving my life," Chief Petty Officer Anthony Phillips said.

He shook Wes's hand now.

"You must be his boy," Anthony Phillips said. "He used to talk about you all the time, what a great basketball player and an even better kid."

"You want to thank my dad for saving your life?" Wes said.

"I never did it right when we were together," Phillips said. "That man is a hero."

Wes stared at him and said, "You know what happened."

"Yeah," he said. "I sure do."

Wes's mom asked him to please come inside with them.

As they walked together toward the front door, Phillips said, "Will the lieutenant be along?"

"No," Wes's mom said.

She took out her key and unlocked the door. As she did, Wes was thinking that maybe the door wasn't the only thing that would be unlocked today.

At last.

Wes and Petty Officer Phillips followed her inside. It took Petty Officer Phillips a long time to tell the story about what happened to them and their unit that day. It involved a place called Kabul in Afghanistan, and it involved Navy SEALs fighting, as Wes knew they did, against the Taliban.

"We were supposed to be advising and assisting at the time," Petty Officer Phillips said. "But it wasn't very long before we were doing a lot more than that. We were protecting and we were proud to do it.

"Your dad was our leader. He always maintained his cool, especially under pressure," Phillips said. "We all looked up to him. But one of the guys in our unit was a hothead. Jake was his name, Jake Thompson. Jake looked up to your dad, too, but he sometimes acted like he was playing a video game and the lieutenant had to remind him to calm down. It's not easy, being over there. I don't blame Jake. He was just dealing with the danger and the stress like the rest of us. But he and your dad, they sometimes butted heads."

Wes watched Petty Officer Phillips as he spoke. Watched how carefully he was picking his words, as if he wanted to tell the story exactly right. He was taking his time, telling it at his own speed.

"There came a day when we unexpectedly found ourselves in a hot spot. Our radios were down and we didn't know that a group of rebels was in the area. There we were, surrounded by fighters in Humvees and jeeps, badly outnumbered and no way to call for backup."

Petty Officer Phillips took a deep breath. His eyes seemed to be watching something that wasn't there. Then he continued.

"Jake decides on his own to create a diversion. There was this lone Humvee, separate from the others on the perimeter, rocket launchers on the back of it. Jake figured if he could get to it, he could provide cover for the rest of the unit. Maybe buy time until Special Forces got there.

"Your dad, he was in charge of keeping everyone alive, so he tells Jake to stand down. If anyone is going to risk his life to get them out of there, it would be him. Jake wasn't having it, though. He makes off to the Humvee. He takes out the two Taliban guys operating it and climbs in back to where rocket launchers are. That was as far as he got before taking a bullet. The gunfire had given him away and he was a sitting duck out there.

"That's when Lieutenant Davies tells me and the others in the unit to cover him. He wants to get Jake's body, won't let it stay with the Taliban. Trouble is, everyone knows we're there now so the element of surprise is gone. Didn't matter to your dad. He runs like a dart out to that Humvee, no fear. The rest of us, we had his back. He lifts Jake onto his shoulders like he weighs nothing and makes it all the way back to the unit, automatic fire kicking up dirt all around him. By that point, Special Forces arrives in a copter. The lieutenant orders the rest of us to get on board. There's too much weight for all of us to escape, though, and no time to argue. Your dad, he stays behind and single-handedly fights off the Taliban until the copter can return to get him. He took a bullet in the leg just as he was climbing on board. But I guess you already know that part."

Wes and his mom were silent. Wes's heart was beating fast. He looked at his mom. She had tears running down her face.

"Like I said, Lieutenant Davies is a hero. Yet all he could talk about was how he had lost a man, how he'd let down Jake."

Wes finally found his voice. "That's what Dad was talking about that day I found him in the park," he said. "I didn't understand what he meant at the time. But as he walked away, he said that being a team guy wasn't supposed to get people killed."

Now he knew why, and how, his dad had been dying a little bit at a time ever since he got back from Afghanistan.

That's what had been killing him.

THIRTY-THREE

BEFORE PETTY OFFICER PHILLIPS LEFT, he gave them his phone number, his email address, and his home address in Bethesda. He said he still wanted to see Wes's dad and thank him in person for saving his life. When Wes's mom explained what Lt. Michael Davies had been like since coming back from Afghanistan, Petty Officer Phillips said, "We have to do for him what he did for us."

"Wes and I feel the same way," Christine Davies said.

"I want to be there for him," Phillips said. "And if the rest of the guys who served with him knew what he was going through, they'd feel the same way."

Wes's mom smiled.

"Thank you for your service," she said.

Wes knew she said that to every single member of the military she encountered in her life.

"People say you're either brave or you're not," Phillips said to her. "I'm not so sure about that. I think a lot of what I learned about being brave I learned from your husband."

He shook hands with Wes's mom. Then he did the same with Wes.

"He'll be okay," he said. "He's got the two of you. He's got everything inside him that made him lead and the rest of us follow. All he used to talk about was getting back with the two of you. Now he needs to do that again."

Petty Officer Phillips left.

Wes said, "We need to go find Dad right now."

"How about we sit down for a second and talk?" she said.

He followed her into the living room. The two of them sat on the couch, turning till they were facing each other. She took both of Wes's hands into hers and squeezed them.

"Now we know for sure why your dad is the way he is," she said. "But that doesn't mean we know how to help him put himself back together. He's still broken. Or at least broken up."

"But we have to tell him that nobody blames him for what happened!" Wes blurted out.

"Your dad knows that in his heart, because he's too smart not to," she said. "But admitting that to himself and accepting it are two different things."

"*Please*, Mom," Wes said. "*Please* let's go find him."

She was still holding his hands, as if afraid that if she let go, Wes might go running out the front door. But then she surprised him.

"Okay," she said.

She pulled her phone out of the back pocket of her jeans,

tapped on it with her index finger. Held it to her ear. Shook her head.

"Straight to voice mail," she said.

Wes pulled out his own phone and tapped out a text message to his dad:

Dad. Please call. Important. Wes

Then he hit send.

"He hasn't replied to one of my texts in a long time," Wes said. "But I have to try."

"Let's take a ride over to his apartment," she said.

"What if he's not there?" Wes said. "Or if he's there and doesn't answer the door?"

"If he doesn't answer, we'll stop by the one bar he told me he likes to go to," she said. "I found him there one time."

"You didn't tell me," Wes said. "What happened when you did?"

"It didn't go well," she said. "He told me that I didn't belong, and to please not ever show up there again."

"If he's there today, it will be different," Wes said.

"And why is that?"

"Because I'll be with you," Wes said.

Michael Davies didn't answer the door at the Woodside Garden Apartments. Wes rang the bell and banged on the door. It was the same as the other time he'd come here. Nothing.

"Let's go to the bar," Wes said.

"There's a lot of bars, honey," she said.

"Let's at least try that one," he said.

It was called the Fado Irish Pub. They saw the long bar when they got inside, television sets above it showing different college basketball games, and a room with tables apart from the bar area called the Dublin Room, where people were still having lunch.

Wes and his mom walked around the front room, and then into the dining area. But there was no sign of his dad.

Before they left, Wes's mom went up to the bartender, took out her phone, and showed him one of the pictures of Wes's dad she had on it.

"I think my husband is in here frequently," she said.

The bartender looked at her phone, and smiled.

"Lieutenant Mike," he said. "He was in here a couple of hours ago."

"Was he drinking?"

"Cheeseburger and a Coke," the bartender said. "Didn't even finish the burger. Said he had to be somewhere."

"Did he happen to mention where?" Christine Davies said.

"Yeah, as a matter of fact he did," the bartender said. "Him and the other guy said they had to get to their game."

THIRTY-FOUR

I N THE CAR, WES SAID to his mom, "Dad had to get to a game? Did he ever mention being on a team?"

"No," she said. "And the bartender said he didn't know the other man."

"Maybe he'll explain it to us the next time we see him," Wes said. "Whenever that is."

So, on a day when one mystery had been solved—what had happened to Lt. Michael Davies in Kabul—another one had taken its place.

What game? Wes thought.

Wes sent one more text message to his dad and then gave up. His mom left one more voice-mail message, and then she gave up.

"When he's ready to talk, he will," she said. "We just have to continue to be patient."

"I'm about as good at that as I am at talking about stuff," Wes said.

It got a smile out of her.

"Wow," she said. "That's not good."

"It's true."

"So is something else," she said. "While we wait for him to be back in our lives, we have to keep living our own."

So Wes did that. He went to school. He went to practice. He was always happy to be there, happy that things were so much better with Dinero, even though he thought Dinero was quieter than usual this week, distant not just from Wes, but the other guys on the team, too.

As they were leaving Thursday night's practice Wes said to him, "You okay?"

Maybe I *can* talk about stuff, Wes thought, as long as it's not about me.

"Yeah," Dinero said. "All good."

"You sure?"

"Just a little jammed up with school stuff," Dinero said.

"Anything I can do to help?" Wes said.

Dinero smiled, as if what they were talking about was no big deal.

"Just keep helping me with basketball," he said. "I gotta handle schoolwork on my own."

They were in the lobby of the rec center. They heard the quick burst of a car horn.

"My dad," Dinero said. He started to walk across the lobby, then turned and said to Wes, "How are things with your dad?"

"Same," he said.

"Sorry," Dinero said.

175

"Me too," Wes said.

Dinero shook his head. "Dads," he said, and then was gone.

Emmanuel came up from behind Wes. They were going home with his parents tonight.

"Something up with the Money Man?" E said.

"Maybe," Wes said. "But whatever it is, he didn't want to talk about it."

"Things still cool between the two of you?"

"Don't know why they wouldn't be," Wes said.

Sometimes you didn't know what you didn't know.

THIRTY-FIVE

THEIR GAME ON SATURDAY WAS against Prince George's County, second of the regular season against the Pistons, in their gym, the White Oak Community Rec Center, in Silver Spring.

There were two games left in the regular season, and the Hawks were still alone in first place. The Pistons were in second, the Montgomery County Grizzlies third, Potomac Valley fourth. The Hawks still had just one loss. But nobody in the group bunched behind them had more than three, so a lot could change with seeding before the top four teams made the league tournament, which would send its champ to the nationals in South Carolina.

A lot had changed since the start of the season, in Wes's life and on his team. But the goals were still the same:

Be the best team.

Be seen.

And what better place to be seen, as you got yourself ready for the next level, than at the National Travel Basketball Association tournament?

But Wes knew better than to get ahead of himself. It was

another thing his dad had always drummed into him. Take your eye off the ball and somebody will steal it from you.

The only thing you could control was the game you were playing. That meant the one today against the Pistons, and their point guard, Tate Brooks, and Matt Riley, the same small forward that Wes had gone up against last time the two teams had played.

Matt, whose hair looked even redder than Wes remembered it, came over to say hi right before the game started.

"Our point guard says this game today is gonna be different than it was last time," he said.

Wes grinned, bumped him some fist, and said, "Dude, that's the fun of it. They're *all* different."

"Things more chill than they were before between you and *your* point guard?" Matt asked.

Wes knew he meant *chill* in a good way.

"It's why we're looking to run hot," Wes said.

And the Hawks *did* run hot from the start, sharing the ball, D-ing up all over the court, fast-breaking every chance they got. Tate was missing his shots. Wes was making Matt miss, forcing him away from his spots, contesting every pass Tate tried to throw to him.

The Hawks were up by ten points at the end of the first quarter, and by sixteen halfway into the second.

It happened then, as if somebody had thrown a switch at the White Oak Rec Center.

The Money Man showed up.

Just like that, it was as if Dinero's trip to Wes's house had never happened. As if the Money Man had never asked Wes to

help him become more of a team man. Just like that—and until
Coach sat Dinero down—they turned into a one-man team.

Again.

Wes thought about what Matt Riley said before the game, about
things being chill between him and Dinero. Well, they were now,
but in the worst way, because Dinero was freezing out everybody
else on the Hawks, except when he needed one of them to be at
the receiving end of a hey-look-at-me pass.

Dinero wasn't just running hot.

He was on fire.

Wes was surprised that it lasted as long as it did, for about
three minutes of game time before Coach Saunders had seen
enough.

And the thing of it was, Dinero was extending the Hawks' lead.
He pulled up on a break, and instead of driving to the basket,
shot a three. It went in. He threw a no-look pass to Russ, and then
another to E. They both made shots. In a blink, he had turned his
matchup with Tate Brooks into a complete *mis*match. Finally, he
took an outlet pass from E, got ahead of everybody, but instead of
shooting a straight layup, he bounced the ball off the backboard
to DeAndre, and he laid the ball in.

The next whistle, Coach pulled him.

Dinero was shocked.

"You're taking me *out*?" he said.

"As a matter of fact, son, I am," Coach said.

"But I can't miss!" Dinero said.

He was being too loud now, the way he'd just been way too
loud in the game.

"What you're missing is the point about what we're trying to do here," Coach said, keeping his own voice down. "We've had this talk, son. We play as a team."

"Scoreboard!" Dinero said, and even pointed at the one closest to them.

"When I only coach by that," Coach said, "then I'll step out the way and let somebody else do this job. Now, turn down the volume and go sit down."

"This is so *wrong*," Dinero said, almost to himself as much as Coach.

"Finally," Coach Saunders said, "we agree on something."

The Hawks were still ahead by sixteen points when the first half ended. The second half began with Dinero still on the bench. Josh took over at point guard, but Wes really played as much point as he did. The Hawks went back to sharing the ball, playing the way they had at the start of the game.

With a minute to go in the third quarter, even the Pistons' shooting guard, Sammy Orr, got hot and cut the Hawks' lead to ten.

Wes gave a quick look at their bench. Dinero was still sitting next to Coach, who was making no move to put him back into the game. Josh hit Wes after Wes made a great backdoor cut. Matt Riley missed. On the last play of the quarter, Casey Fisher released early on a Sammy miss, and Wes threw him a football pass. Casey got a layup right before the horn. The lead was back to fourteen. The Pistons never got closer than that the rest of the way.

Dinero never got off the bench, except for timeouts.

When the game was over, Dinero reluctantly got into the handshake line along with everybody else. He didn't speak to any of the Pistons. He didn't speak to anyone on the court, period. Showed no interest in the homemade cookies that Josh's mom had brought.

He just wanted to get out of there.

But he had to wait, because his father was at the other end of the court with Coach, underneath what had been the Hawks' basket in the second half. Mr. Rey was the one doing most of the talking, as far as Wes could tell. It reminded Wes of the scene between Dinero and his dad after their last game, when he'd given Dinero an earful. Now he was doing it with Coach Saunders.

At one point, Mr. Rey pointed a finger at Coach, who stared at the finger until Mr. Rey put his hand down.

While that was going on, Wes walked over to Dinero and said, "Man, what happened out there today?"

Because he couldn't *not* ask.

Dinero didn't look at Wes. He just kept staring at his dad and Coach, his face telling Wes everything. Mostly about how much Dinero wanted his dad to walk away.

"I don't want to talk about it," Dinero said.

"But what about everything we talked about?" Wes said. "About us being a team?"

"We want the team to win, right?" Dinero said. "Well, wasn't our lead bigger before Coach took me out? Is that a bad thing?"

"Not saying it was," Wes said. "It just wasn't a team thing."

"Sometimes the best thing for this team is me taking over the way I did," Dinero said. "The way I *can*."

It finally ended between Coach and Mr. Rey. Dinero's dad began to walk in their direction, his face red.

"Dude," Wes said. "Talk to me."

"*I can't*," Dinero whispered.

His dad jerked his head in the direction of the doors to the gym and kept walking. Dinero followed him. And all Wes could think was that what had turned into a long day for Dinero Rey was about to get longer.

It was funny, he thought.

For so much of the game, the way they'd played really had been money. It was why they'd won.

It was the Money Man who'd lost.

THIRTY-SIX

WES WAS IN MR. CORREA'S office after school on Monday. His mom was picking him up after that for an early Hawks' practice.

Wes was still trying to understand what had happened with Dinero on Saturday.

"I thought everything was all good," he said to Mr. Correa. "And then it turned into crazytown."

"Sounds like," Mr. Correa said.

"I think it has something to do with his dad," Wes said, and then described how after one game he'd been upset with Dinero even though the Hawks had won, and this time he'd been upset with Coach, even though the Hawks had won.

"It's like he doesn't care how we play," Wes said. "Just how Dinero *looks*."

Wes had never asked Mr. Correa about his private conversations with Dinero and wasn't about to start now.

"I think he's under a lot of pressure from his dad," Wes continued.

"You said you never felt that kind of pressure," Mr. C said. "From your dad, I mean."

"I never felt him pushing me," Wes said. "At least until now. When he keeps pushing me and my mom away."

"Fathers and sons," Mr. Correa said, slowly shaking his head, but smiling. "When my dad was the one doing the pushing, he was pushing me away from basketball and toward baseball."

"No way," Wes said. "You're way too good a basketball player."

"But my dad thought I was a better pitcher. And he thought baseball gave me a better chance to get to the pros. Only I knew something that he didn't, even when I was your age: I was never gonna be good enough to make it to the pros in either sport. He didn't see it that way. He thought baseball was my ticket to fame and fortune."

He pushed back from his desk, put an old-school pair of Adidas high-tops up on his desk, white with blue stripes.

"I have a feeling, just off what you've told me," Mr. C said, "that Dinero's dad thinks Dinero is going to be the next Steph Curry. Or Russell Westbrook. Pick a guard."

Wes turned and picked up the Nerf ball off the floor, then drained a baby hook.

"You may very well be the best Nerf shooter I've ever seen," Mr. C said.

"I would've passed it to you," Wes said, grinning at him. "Only you would have missed."

"Sad, but true," his adviser said.

"At least Dinero's dad is around," Wes said.

"You need to be patient with your dad," Mr. Correa said.

And then it all came spilling out of Wes, everything Petty Officer Phillips had told him about what happened to his dad's unit. How Petty Officer Phillips had come around wanting to thank Wes's dad for something his dad was obviously still blaming himself for.

"If they all know it wasn't his fault, how come he doesn't?" Wes said.

"Give him time," Mr. Correa said. "He'll find his way back to you and your mom."

"I want to believe that," Wes said.

"So, keep believing," Mr. C said. "Basketball is full of momentum swings. It just takes a team a while to find its footing and believe in its shots. Your dad's finding his footing all over again. In time, he'll start believing in himself. And then he's going to need you and your mom like never before. His teammates."

He made a motion with his hands for Wes to pass him the ball. Mr. C shot and even held his follow-through.

Missed.

"Told you," Wes said.

They both laughed. There were so many complications in Wes's life right now, because of his dad and because of Dinero. So much that Wes didn't understand or that didn't make sense to him. But everything always felt right when he was in this office. His problems didn't disappear when he was with Mr. Correa. But they also didn't seem as bad. It was why Wes always walked out of there feeling better.

Mr. Correa believed things would get better with Wes's dad. And because he did, he made Wes believe.

It wasn't all Wes wanted, or even close.

But it would have to do for now.

THIRTY-SEVEN

A COUPLE OF TIMES AT PRACTICE, Wes tried to start conversations with Dinero, as a way of seeing if he was okay. Dinero didn't blow him off when he did or act mean. He just made it clear that he didn't want to talk.

So maybe they were the same in that way.

One time Dinero said to Wes, "I told you I wanted to be more like you. So right now I'm letting my game do the talking. Okay?"

Wes almost told him that his game had practically been shouting at him during the Pistons' game, but didn't.

He just said, "Okay."

They were getting ready to play the last game of the regular season, against Bakari Hogan and the Montgomery County Grizzlies, try to nail down first place in the league once and for all.

"I feel like the playoffs really start today," E said to Wes in the layup line.

"You know what, E?" Wes said to his friend. "I've felt as if every game has been the playoffs for a while."

He leaned in, so he and E could bump shoulders. As always, they were as close as brothers could be. The way Petty Officer Phillips had described the brotherhood of his dad's unit? Wes felt that way about E. And knew that E felt that way about him.

Wes hadn't talked to E or anybody else this week about the way the last game with the Grizzlies had ended, the pass going out of bounds.

All E said to Wes was, "We owe these boys one."

"I owe them one," Wes said, and left it at that.

The Grizzlies won the coin flip, which meant they got the ball first. Before they inbounded the ball, Bakari said to Wes, "Hear you guys have only gotten better since the last time we played."

"You believe everything you hear?" Wes said.

Bakari smiled. He still had his amazing dreadlocks pulled back into a ponytail, still had the high socks and the shooting sleeve.

"Have a good one," he said to Wes.

"You too," Wes said.

He didn't shut down Bakari in the first half. Bakari was way too good for that. But Wes remembered what Bakari liked to do and where he liked to shoot the ball. It wasn't just that Wes remembered how the last Hawks-Grizzlies game had ended. He remembered all of it.

So even though Bakari was getting his points, Wes was making him work for every one of them. When Bakari would miss, Wes would box out like a demon. And even doing all that, Wes was still able to play his best game at the other end. He got hot mid-way through the first quarter, and this time Dinero didn't freeze him out, showing no hesitation as he fed Wes the ball every time he was open.

But E and DeAndre were scoring inside. They were moving and the ball was moving, and a six-point lead at the end of the first quarter had doubled early into the second. It was as if they were trying to make Bakari see what he said he'd heard about the Hawks, that they'd just gotten better and better since the teams' first meeting.

It looked like they might win easily today.

Then Dinero made things hard on himself, and everybody, again.

He pulled up on a break and, instead of passing the ball to Josh, who was wide open, hoisted up a three. Missed. Wes was trailing the ball. Bakari had stayed in the backcourt, thinking that the Hawks were about to get an easy two, not a missed three. Trevor Arrazi, the Grizzlies' power forward, rebounded Dinero's miss, turned and threw the ball the length of the court to Bakari. Lead was down to ten.

On the Hawks' next possession, Dinero dribbled around until he got into the lane, pulling the Grizzlies' big to him. Wes was open in the right corner. But Dinero didn't feed him this time. Instead he tried to throw a bounce pass back between his legs to Russ Adams at the top of the key.

Only the pass was way wide of Russ. The kid guarding Russ picked the ball off, sailed down the court alone, and made the layup that cut the Hawks' lead to eight. Everybody on the Grizzlies' bench jumped up, feeling the game changing in front of their eyes. Coach didn't even wait three minutes this time. He stood up, signaled for a timeout, and put in Josh to replace Dinero.

"You're taking me out for one missed shot and one bad pass?" Dinero said.

Too loud, again.

As if he hadn't learned anything in a week.

"Trying not to let this turn into a bad end to the half for our team," Coach said.

Dinero opened his mouth, then closed it. Maybe he had at least learned when to stop talking between last Saturday and this one.

He sat for the rest of the half. The Hawks and Grizzlies played even until the horn. The Hawks' lead was still eight.

It was then that somebody's dad made a scene at the rec center. Only this time it wasn't Wes's dad.

Mr. Rey didn't come out of the stands screaming the way Michael Davies had that time. But as soon as the horn did sound, he headed straight for Coach Saunders again.

"I'd like a word with you," Mr. Rey said.

"I'm sorry," Coach said, keeping his voice even, "but it is not appropriate for you to approach me during a game. I'm not sure it was even appropriate for you to approach me after the game, the way you did last week. But we are most definitely not going to have this conversation now. So it will have to wait."

"It can't wait," Mr. Rey said, "if you're planning to bench my son for the rest of this game."

Wes looked around. Everybody in the gym was staring at

Coach and Dinero's dad.

"The way I coach this team is my business, sir," Coach said. "And that means coaching them in a way that I think is best for them."

"I have a problem with you continuing to make him look bad," Mr. Rey said.

He wasn't screaming. But his voice was getting louder.

"With all due respect, Mr. Rey," Coach said, "I believe the one who has created the problem for your son is you."

"What is that supposed to mean?"

"It means that I believe you are telling him to play basketball in a way that is contrary to our best interests and to his own."

Wes looked over at Dinero, who seemed as frozen in place as Wes had been the day his dad had been the one to come out of the stands.

"Well, then," Mr. Rey said, unwilling or unable to back down, "maybe the best thing for my son, and for your team, is for me to take him home right now."

"*No!*" Dinero yelled.

"No," a man's voice said from behind them.

Wes turned around and saw his own dad standing there.

"You don't want to do this to your boy," Lt. Michael Davies said to Mr. Rey. "And you don't want to do it to yourself."

THIRTY-EIGHT

HE WASN'T WEARING HIS ORIOLES cap today.

And he had shaved his beard. His blue Navy hoodie looked brand-new to Wes. So did the pressed khaki pants he was wearing.

He wasn't loud today. He wasn't weaving from side to side. Wes didn't know where he'd been watching from in the gym.

But here he was.

"Who are you?" Mr. Rey said.

Lt. Michael Davies gave a brief nod in Wes's direction.

"I'm *his* dad," he said.

"This isn't your concern," Mr. Rey said.

"Actually," Wes's dad said, "it is."

Mr. Rey said, "This is about my son."

"No," Wes's dad said. "It's not just about your son. It's about mine, too. It's about the team. And what's best for the team."

Somehow, while this was going on, Dinero had come over so

he was standing right next to Wes. Michael Davies nodded again, at both of them.

"The two of them being a team is what's best for them and for the whole team," he said.

Wes knew it had to be getting close to the time when the second half was supposed to start. He saw Coach Saunders look over to where the two refs were standing at half-court. The taller of the two refs, Mr. Costello, who had worked a lot of Hawks' games this season, just smiled at Coach and made a motion with his hand that said, Go ahead.

Maybe they knew that what was happening over near the Hawks' bench might be as important as the game.

Or more important.

Coach and Mr. Rey and Wes's dad had formed a small circle now. Coach turned and told his players to go start warming up for the second half. But when Wes and Dinero went to join them, Coach told them to stay.

"Listen to Lieutenant Davies," Coach said to Mr. Rey. "He's explaining things as well as I ever could."

"You're holding my son back," Mr. Rey said to Coach.

He had finally lowered his voice. Maybe it was because of the presence of Wes's dad. Maybe, Wes thought, being able to command respect was something you never lost.

No matter how hard you tried.

"Something's holding your boy back," Michael Davies said. "But from what I'm seeing, it's not Coach here. All I ever see him doing is trying to coach your boy and all of them the right way."

"He sits him down every time he tries to have a little fun," Mr. Rey said. "It's like he doesn't understand the modern game." He shook his head, almost in a stubborn way. "And he sure doesn't understand how he's messing with my son's future."

"Your son is a wonderful player," Wes's dad said. "Same as my son is. But the best way to have a future in this game is by making everybody around you better. That's how you become your own best self."

"I don't need somebody telling me what's best for my son," Mr. Rey said.

He wasn't backing up at all.

Michael Davies smiled.

"What I've found," he said, "is that sometimes the best thing is to let them teach us."

Coach quietly said, "We need to start the second half."

Wes's dad nodded in agreement, but then looked at Dinero's dad.

"What I think is the best thing for everybody right now is for you to come up into the stands and watch the rest of the game with me," he said.

Mr. Rey said, "Is my son going to play?"

"Sure," Coach said, making it sound like the most obvious thing in the world. "Who knows, we might just now be moving up on the good parts."

Mr. Rey turned and stared at Lt. Michael Davies. But Wes could see the fight and the anger had gone out of him.

"Let's go," Dinero's dad said, and then started walking

around the bench and up into the stands, as if he were the one taking the lead. But as Wes's dad started to follow him, Coach stopped him by putting a hand on his shoulder.

"In all ways," Coach said to him, "thank you for your service."

THIRTY-NINE

THE HAWKS PLAYED WELL AT the start of the third quarter. But the Grizzlies played better. Much better.

Wes missed a few open shots. Dinero made one spectacular double-crossover move, got inside, blew by the Grizzlies' bigs. And missed a layup he could usually make with his eyes closed.

"I'm an idiot," Dinero said as he and Wes were getting back on defense.

"It'll go in next time," Wes said.

Wes was doing all the things that had worked against Bakari in the first half, but nothing worked because Bakari had just gone off. He and Wes were still the same guys. But it was a different game now. Wes knew why: It was basketball and Bakari had found his shot.

Bakari went left a couple of times when Wes was certain he was going right. A couple of minutes later he seemed to have a good look, but suddenly spun, backed Wes up, and banked home a turnaround, a shot Wes hadn't seen from him in either game they'd played this season.

Really what he'd done was raise his game. Now Wes would have to do the same.

But the Grizzlies had momentum and came all the way back to tie the game. Even with the game tied, they seemed to be winning.

The teams traded points and were still tied with two and a half minutes left. Grizzlies' ball. Bakari made a sweet pass inside to Trevor, but E got a block. Immediately, Wes released. E threw as accurate a long pass as he had all season. It had to be accurate because Bakari was running stride for stride with Wes. If the ball had come up a little short, Bakari would have intercepted it. He didn't. Wes got a layup.

Hawks by two.

Trevor made a turnaround of his own against E.

Game tied again, 48–all.

Dinero had a great look at a three, but at the last second he kicked the ball inside to DeAndre, who had a much better look, about six feet away. DeAndre made the shot. Hawks by two again. Bakari, even with Wes all over him, made a long two-pointer, his foot just inside the three-point line. Game tied at 50. Wes tried a three from the right corner. Was sure he'd knocked it down. Watched in amazement as the ball rattled out.

Game still tied, Grizzlies' ball.

Wes hounded Bakari into passing the ball to Trevor, who shot from just inside the free-throw line. The shot was too strong, bouncing off the back of the rim and right into E's hands.

Twenty seconds left.

Hawks' ball.

Coach called time.

"Two-man game," he said to Wes and Dinero.

"But what's the play?" Dinero said.

"The play is you two playing a two-man game and figuring it out," Coach said.

As they walked back out on the court, Dinero whispered to Wes, "I'll get it to you."

Wes gave a quick shake of his head.

"That's what they'll be expecting," he said. "Especially Bakari."

"You want me to take the shot?" Dinero said.

Wes knew he didn't have much time. The ref was waiting with the ball, side out.

"Take your guy off the dribble," he said into Dinero's ear. "Give it over to me. But I'll fake the shot. When I give it back, you put that move on them again and beat everybody to the basket."

"You're our best shot," Dinero said.

"Nope," Wes said. "You are."

Wes was on the left wing this time when Dinero threw him the ball. Wes put the ball on the floor, as if he were trying to put a move on Bakari, get himself into position to take the shot to win the game.

He dribbled left, toward the left corner, and immediately created some space for himself.

But before he got to the corner, he stopped and jumped and fired the ball back to Dinero Rey, who was just to the left of the free-throw line.

Ten seconds left.

Right-handed dribble from Dinero. Then switching to his left hand. Then back to his right, in a blur.

Seven.

Dinero had the step he needed on Tate.

Trevor left E and tried to cut him off. Trevor, who looked like a tall, skinny tree when he had his arms up in the air.

Five seconds.

Dinero gave him his hesitation step.

Released the ball with two seconds showing on the clock.

The ball didn't go over Trevor's hands. It went around them.

Right to E, who was all alone in front of the hoop.

Bucket.

Buzzer.

FORTY

THERE WAS ONLY ONE THING wrong with the picture after Wes and the guys were out of the handshake line and had begun their celebration with one another:

When he looked up to the top of the stands, where his dad and Dinero's dad had sat for the second half, only Mr. Rey was there, starting to make his way back to the court, even smiling for a change.

Even as Wes felt the smile disappearing from his own face because his dad had somehow managed to disappear as quickly as he'd appeared in the first place.

He went over to where his mom was standing with E's parents.

"He left?" Wes said.

"He did."

"Just like that?" Wes said. "Without saying good-bye to me?"

"He said he had an appointment he could not miss," she said. "But he promised he'd explain later."

"Sounds like it was an appointment more important than the one he could have had with me after the game," Wes said.

"I don't think that's so."

"I do," he said.

"Your dad came back a long way today," Christine Davies said. "You saw how he took charge of the situation at halftime. That was the husband I know, and the father you knew."

"He could have at least waited to say good-bye," Wes said.

"He took charge today and then you took charge in your game," she said. "Let's focus on the positives. Okay?"

"Okay," he said.

His dad had been there today, for Wes and Dinero and the team. Even for Mr. Rey, whether Mr. Rey had liked it at first or not. That wasn't nothing.

But where had he gone?

What *was* more important than Wes and his game?

E came over later and they watched college basketball on television, and then E stayed for dinner, Wes's mom having told E's parents that she'd be happy to drive him home.

"I felt like we were in a movie when your dad just showed up like that," E said to Wes.

"Wish I knew how the movie's going to come out," Wes said.

They were still at the table, eating the banana splits Wes's mom had made for them.

"Be patient," his mom said. "Aren't you always telling me that you've got to let a play develop?"

"You sound like Mr. Correa with that patience stuff," he said.

"An example of great minds thinking alike," she said.

"Admit something," E said. "You're at least allowing yourself to feel good about yourself and Dinero and our team?"

"Our team, mostly," Wes said.

"You could have taken the last shot if you wanted to," E said. "Admit *that*, too."

"Doesn't matter whether I could have or not," Wes said. "Dinero ended up with a better shot."

"We *were* a team today when we had to be," E said.

"And my dad had a hand in that," Wes said.

"Didn't he, though?" his mom said.

Wes took the ride with his mom to E's house when it was time for E to leave. On the way they talked about maybe going over to the rec center for open gym tomorrow.

Wes did some reading when he got home, a book about a New York City point guard who ended up becoming kind of a hoop legend when he and his mom moved to California. But by the time he'd read ten pages, he could feel his eyes getting heavy. He had gotten that tired, that fast, as if the whole day had caught up with him.

He washed his face, brushed his teeth, shut out the lights, yelled out to his mom that he loved her. She yelled back that she loved him more.

But he was still thinking about his dad and where he'd gone after the game. What he might be doing right this minute. Was he watching a game at that bar? Did he still even watch basketball games at night the way he used to?

Was he missing Wes and his mom as much as they missed him?

Wes didn't see the text Mr. Correa had sent him until the next morning.

Meet me at the gym at Annapolis Christian, one o'clock.
Good game.

FORTY-ONE

WES'S MOM DROVE HIM OVER to Annapolis Christian and said she'd come in to say hello to Mr. Correa. Wes had brought his game sneaks and his gym bag with a couple of bottles of water in it, and even his Hawks' shooting shirt, just because he was proud of it.

But Mr. Correa hadn't invited him to play; he found that out as soon as he walked into the gym.

The court was filled with kids that had to be the third-graders that he'd told Wes he was coaching on weekends, sometimes on both Saturdays and Sundays, depending on gym schedules.

This had to be one of those Sundays.

"I thought when he said to show up for a good game, he meant one I could play in," Wes said.

His mom grinned. "Looks like you'd dominate if you did," she said.

"You can go, Mom," Wes said. "Mr. C must have wanted me to come watch his kids."

"Maybe I'll watch for a little while, too," she said. "And remember what it was like when your rug-rat team was playing another."

They'd played four minutes already, according to the score-board, but the score was only 2–2. Mr. Correa's bench was at the far end. He was standing in front of it, because one of his players had just used what looked like all of his strength to get the ball to the basket and score.

"Way to go, Danny," Mr. Correa said, smiling and shaking a fist at him.

It wasn't until he sat back down that Wes and his mom saw what Mr. C must have wanted them to see:

Wes's dad, who'd been sitting right behind him.

"*Mom*," Wes said.

"I see," she said.

"What's he doing here?"

"Coaching," she said.

They were in the corner and sat down now in the first row of the bleachers. Wes's dad stood up as they did, smiling himself, waving Mr. C's players to get back on defense.

Now they knew what game he'd left the bar for, and where he must have been going after Wes's own game the day before. He didn't have a game to play. He had one to coach. He was so wrapped up in what he was doing, and so happy doing it, that he didn't seem to notice Wes and his mom. Or didn't let on that he did.

Wes watched him and thought:

He looks like he's home.

Or maybe almost home.

It wasn't until halftime that Mr. Correa and Wes's dad walked down to where Wes and his mom were sitting.

"Busted," Michael Davies said.

"Blame me," Mr. Correa said. "I asked them to come."

"You didn't mention that to me," Wes's dad said.

"Well, yeah," Mr. C said, shrugging. "But until now I'd failed to mention that I gave you a coaching job, even if the only pay is cookies and juice boxes when the game is over."

"Hey," Wes's dad said to his mom.

"Hey yourself," she said. "We having any fun yet?"

"Ton of it," he said.

Wes looked at Mr. C.

"How did this happen?" he said.

"I'll explain after the game," he said. "For now, I gotta get back to work."

"It doesn't look like work to me," Wes said.

Mr. Correa grinned. "Are you kidding?" he said. "Trying to make me look as if I know what I'm doing is a huge job."

The score was 8–6 for Mr. C's team by then. There were times in the third quarter when Wes honestly thought that neither team might score a single basket. But the kids were having a great time running up and down the court, and Wes was having a great time watching, because they did make him remember what it was like when he first started playing organized ball, and could barely remember the final score an hour after he got home.

What Wes remembered best about those games was that he'd be afraid to look up at the clock during the second half, because he didn't want to know when the game would be ending, way too soon for him. The only thing that made him sad at eight wasn't losing, it was knowing that when the game was over, he had to wait a whole week to play another one.

But as the clock started to run out today, he found himself watching his dad more than the players. Michael Davies would usually pick out one boy to talk to during a timeout, get down on a knee, smiling and talking away, pointing to the court. Sometimes he'd call out one of the players' names and simply point them in the right direction. It never sounded to Wes like he was ordering them around. More like he was making suggestions.

A couple of times he called out to the team—by now Wes knew the name was Warriors—and made a motion like he was reminding them to box out after a missed shot.

One time, Wes leaned over to his mom and said, "He looks as young as anybody out there."

"Doesn't he," she said.

The game ended up tied at 12 with twenty seconds left. So, it turned out that the Hawks weren't the only ones playing a close game this weekend. Mr. Correa, still smiling, called a timeout and waved his players over. They sprinted to the bench. When they got there, he pointed to Wes's dad, who knelt in the middle of the circle of third-graders, talking away, finally pointing at the boy Mr. C had called Danny and the tallest kid on the team, clearly drawing up a play he thought could win them the day.

"Back door," Wes said to his mom.

"I'm going to assume that's not the way you want us to leave when the game is over," she said.

"Mom," he said.

"Sorry," she said.

"Dad loves that play," Wes said. "The blond boy, Danny, is the one who's handled the ball most of the time. The tall boy with the freckles has scored most of their points. Danny will be on one side. The tall guy will be on the other. He'll come running out, maybe even wave for Danny to throw the ball. But then he'll stop, and cut back to the basket—going through the back door on the play—and Danny will try to throw him the ball."

"I actually followed that," she said.

"If it works right, they'll win the game," Wes said.

"You're sure of this?" his mom said.

"Not that it'll work," Wes said. "I just know how Dad likes the game to be played."

It worked.

Danny waited until the exact right moment, as Wes was sure he'd been told, and threw a high pass over the defense, though it didn't have to be all that high considering the ages and heights of the players. The tall, skinny boy caught the ball, dribbled twice, didn't travel, and made the layup that won the game for the Warriors.

After he did, the Warriors' players on the court came running for Wes's dad, all of them trying to high-five him at once.

"He looks pretty happy," Wes's mom said.

"So do you," Wes said.

"I don't think it's about winning the game," she said.

"It never was."

They drove back to the house together.

FORTY-TWO

THEY SAT AT THE KITCHEN table, the way they used to after Wes's games. This time Wes's mom joined him and his dad. She drank tea. His dad had a cup of coffee in front of him. Wes said he didn't need anything, he was fine.

Because he was.

They had been talking for a while. Wes's dad had done most of the talking.

"I finally decided I couldn't go on the way I was," he was saying now. "The low point, it goes without saying, was the day I made that awful scene after your game, son, for which I will always be sorry."

"You don't have to apologize to me, Dad," Wes said.

"Yes," he said. "Yes, I do. To both of you."

"But if that day brought you to this one," Christine Davies said, "then maybe it wasn't the worst thing that will ever happen to this family."

His dad sipped his coffee, then said to his wife that she still made a damn fine cup of coffee. She said that he always said that. Didn't make it any less true, he said. Wes watched them and thought: This is the way things used to be, even though he was smart enough to know that they weren't here to talk about his mom's coffee.

"Anthony Phillips came here to see us," Wes's mom said.

"I know," his dad said. "We finally talked."

He looked at them. "He told you the story that I just told you," he said. "He did my job for me."

"All it means," Wes's mom said, "is that you taught him well. And that he's still as loyal to you back here as he was over there."

"Dealing with what happened and Jake's death," Michael Davies said, "turned out to be a different kind of war, just one inside me. It's taken me a long time to figure that out."

He sighed and shook his head. "I decided I could handle it myself," he said.

"You would," Wes's mom said.

She reached across the table, almost without thinking or by force of habit, and put her hand over her husband's.

"But the more Jake's death tore me up, the more I drank," he said.

He looked at Wes. "These things might be hard for you to hear," he said. "But they're harder for me to say."

"I can handle it," Wes said.

"No doubt," his dad said.

He sighed again and kept going.

"But I figured out that I'd had enough," he said. "Not all problem drinkers come to that realization. But I finally did. My drinking wasn't solving problems. It was creating more." He smiled, but it wasn't a happy one. "But I don't have to tell either one of you that."

The kitchen was suddenly quiet. Wes's mom got up and walked to the counter and came back with the pot and poured more coffee for Wes's dad.

When she sat back down, Wes said to his dad, "How the heck did you and Mr. Correa get together?"

He smiled.

"Basketball," he said.

He said he was shooting around one night at the outdoor court near the rec center. Mr. Correa had finished the one practice a week he had with his third-graders. Mr. C remembered Wes telling him about the court and about how Wes and his dad used to shoot there, and how Wes had found his dad there after he'd come out of the stands that day.

"Mr. Correa asked if I wanted some company," Wes's dad said. "Usually I didn't. I went there to be alone. But he just has this way about him."

Wes grinned.

"Tell me about it," he said.

Wes saw his mom shaking her head. "The brotherhood of basketball," she said. "Sometimes I think it's stronger than the ocean."

"It finally worked for Dinero and me," Wes said.

"With a little help from your dad," his mom said.

When Mr. Correa and Michael Davies finished shooting around that night, they went for coffee. And talked for a long time.

"By the end of the night," Wes's dad said, "I felt like your adviser had become mine. He wanted to know if I was seeing a therapist. I told him I was, but not as often as the therapist wanted. He looked at me and said, 'You're a born leader. And now you're not following your best instincts.'"

"And that hit home," Wes's mom said.

"And helped me come home," his dad said.

"Because he found you playing ball that night," Christine Davies said.

"If it weren't that night, it would have been another," he said. "I mattered to him because Wes matters to him."

"And he asked you to help him coach those kids," Wes's mom said.

"He said it would be a different kind of therapy," Michael Davies said.

He asked Mr. Correa not to tell Wes what they were doing or even that they had become friends. He knew that it was going to take basketball to start healing him. But he had stopped drinking by then. And started seeing his therapist at the Naval Academy twice a week. He said he imagined himself as a prizefighter who'd gotten knocked down and nearly knocked out. First he had to get to one knee. Then he had to stand up.

"I knew the only way I wanted to come back to the two of you," he said, "was with clear eyes and a clear head."

"And you didn't know we were coming to the game today until we showed up?" Wes said.

"That was your adviser advising me again," his dad said. "Just without telling me he was doing it."

"Mr. Correa," his mom said, "really is as cool as you say he is."

Wes's dad had talked about clear eyes. He fixed them on Wes.

"I'm not all the way back yet," he said.

"All that matters," Wes said to his dad, "is that you're here."

FORTY-THREE

I T WAS WEIRD, WES THOUGHT, how things worked out sometimes and made you change your dreams.

All he had thought about, from the time the season started, was playing well enough to really be seen this season by his team-mates and coach and opponents, and especially AAU coaches. But even more than that, he kept believing that playing well enough would bring his dad back to him.

But now his dad was back, and living at home again, having moved out of the Woodside Garden Apartments. And it really had nothing to do with the way Wes had played ball or the team man he'd tried to be or the way his team had won, and every-thing to do with a fight his dad had won—and planned to keep winning—inside himself.

Wes still had dreams of playing AAU ball, if the team and the coach and the situation were right. Every once in a while, but never until after a game, Coach Saunders would tell him that an

AAU coach, or two, had been in attendance. But Wes and his parents had been talking a lot about all that the past couple of weeks, how a lot of famous players had done fine on their way to college ball without ever playing a minute in an AAU game.

"You just keep playing the way you're playing," his dad said, "and I have a feeling that things will work out."

When Wes really thought about it, he figured he might have never learned more about basketball and about what it took to be a winner than he'd known at the start of the season. It was because of everything he'd been through. He had learned a lot about getting knocked down. But he knew he'd learned a whole lot more because of the way he'd kept getting back up.

Now there was only one more game left to win, the one that would send them to the travel basketball tournament in South Carolina. That part of his dream hadn't changed. All the Hawks had to do was beat Bakari Hogan and the Montgomery County Grizzlies today in the championship game at the rec center.

The Grizzlies had beaten the Pistons in their semifinals, in the matchup between the teams that had finished second and third in the league. The Hawks had beaten the Potomac Valley Rockets the previous Saturday, and pretty easily, to advance themselves.

At breakfast that morning Wes said to his dad, "I want this one pretty badly, not gonna lie."

"Gee," his dad said, "you've kept that pretty hidden."

"Funny."

"Just don't want it *too* badly," Michael Davies said. "Because when that happens, even to good players, it makes them play bad."

He had already finished the pancakes in record time that his mom had made for him. But it was still way too early to head over to the rec center, because the championship game wasn't starting until one o'clock.

"This is the way it should be, though," Wes said to his dad. "They beat us once, we beat them, today is the rubber match."

His dad grinned. "At which point," he said, "the rubber will meet the road."

"That guy Bakari is really something," Wes said.

"So are you," his dad said. "Just sayin'."

Wes checked his phone, which told him it was only ten minutes later than the last time he'd checked. His dad watched him do it again, then told him to go put on his outdoor sneakers—they were going for a ride.

They went to their park near the rec center to shoot around.

"Just shooting," Wes's dad said when they were walking to the court from the car. "Not looking to tire out the Hawks' star player."

"One of them," Wes said.

"The team is gonna be the star today," his dad said.

"It's not just Bakari," Wes said. "All those guys are good."

"And it's like I've told you your whole basketball life," his dad said. "You wouldn't want it any other way. And shouldn't want it any other way."

Michael Davies said he'd rebound. Wes noticed as soon as they started that his dad was still limping slightly. Maybe he always would be. But he didn't seem to be in any pain today. Of any kind.

His dad fed him the ball. Wes slowly began to move around

the perimeter and do what he'd always been taught to do: take shots he planned to take in the game. Right corner. Foul line. Left corner. Three-pointers from both wings. Not tiring himself out. But feeling a good sweat coming on. Feeling himself getting ready. Knowing he was better off here than he would have been sitting at home, checking his phone.

"Looking good," his dad said after Wes made a shot from the right side that they both knew was three-point distance.

"Feeling good," Wes said.

"I think," his dad said, "that being here is a more productive use of your time."

What they were really doing, Wes knew, without either one of them saying it, was making up for *lost* time. This was the way things used to be. This was the way things were *supposed* to be between them. Wes didn't know how much basketball had brought them back together. But right now, today, it made him feel as connected to his dad as he'd ever been.

"Remember," his dad said. "You take your guy away from where he likes to go and then beat him to the place where you want to be."

"Got it," Wes said.

"And think like a point guard," his dad said.

"Always."

They only stayed at the court for about half an hour. Before they left, Wes said they should switch jobs, and he stood under the basket and rebounded for his dad and fed him the ball. He could see that Lt. Michael Davies had lost a step. More than a step. But he could still shoot the rock.

Wes had all of his game stuff in the car. At about eleven thirty, his dad said it was time to go over to the rec center. As they walked in that direction, Wes's dad put a hand on his shoulder.

"There will be a moment today when you'll know even your best isn't good enough," he said to Wes. "You'll need a little more than that."

"You've told me that since I was the same age those kids you and Mr. C are coaching," Wes said.

His dad stopped then and closed his eyes and smiled. In a quiet voice he said, "It's like a friend of mine told me once: You know I'm right."

They kept walking toward the rec center, only stopping long enough for Wes to pick up his bag with his game sneakers and uniform inside.

Then it was time for him to go inside and play the big game.

FORTY-FOUR

WES HAD NEVER SEEN THE stands at the rec center as full as they were today. They'd even set up a few rows of folding chairs in the corners to handle the overflow.

"All these people here to see if we can win ourselves a fun-filled trip to South Carolina," E said to Wes in the layup line.

"I've never been to South Carolina," Wes said.

"I've never been to *North* Carolina!" E said.

"You worry about geography," Wes said. "I'm gonna go ahead and focus on winning the game."

E grinned. "I'm doing the same," he said. "At the end of the game, I want us to be north of the Grizzlies and them south of us." He put out his hand for a low five. "See what I did there?" he said.

"I know you're just trying to keep me loose," Wes said.

"Always," his best friend said.

Wes's mom and dad were sitting together. Dinero's parents were right behind them. It was, according to Dinero, the first time his mom had been to a game all season. He said that she was too nervous to come and watch him play, but today she was too nervous *not* to watch him play.

"That makes no sense," Wes said to Dinero.

Dinero smiled. His smile had been back lately. A lot.

"Why don't you go over there and explain that to her," he said.

A few minutes before one o'clock, Wes saw Mr. Correa walk through the double doors and start making his way to where Wes's mom and dad were sitting.

Wes ran over to greet him.

"I just wanted to thank you again for everything you did for me this season," Wes said. "And for our family."

"Doesn't make me any less jealous of you," Mr. C said.

"Jealous?" Wes said.

"Yeah," he said, "that you have a game like this to play today and all I get to do is watch."

Wes ran back to where his teammates were taking their last warmup shots, grabbed a ball, dribbled into the right corner, and made a three. Always end up with a make.

Then the Hawks went over and gathered around Coach Joe Saunders.

"The best thing about our team is that we know who we are by now," Coach said. "And the reason we know who we are is because we know the kind of ball we're capable of."

He slowly looked around at his players.

"We owed them one the last time we played them," he said. "Now they feel as if they owe us one."

He was smiling now.

"They think they're the best team in the league," he said. "But they only *think* that. So, we got them there. Because we *know* we're the best doggoned team in this league. Now we just got to take care of our business and prove it one more time."

He put his hand out in the center of the circle. The Hawks leaned in and put their hands on top of his.

"Sometimes in sports you're exactly where you're supposed to be. And right now you boys are exactly where *you're* supposed to be."

He smiled again, and looked around, without taking his hand away, and said in a soft voice, "Go Hawks."

"*Go Hawks!*" his players shouted back at him.

As Wes and Dinero walked out to the court, Dinero said, "Let's do this."

"Let's," Wes said.

Dinero smiled. "One more thing? Keep your head up."

"Got it," Wes said.

He looked at the clock.

One o'clock, straight up.

At last.

By one fifteen, the Hawks were down 12–2.

Wes had always talked about basketball as a miss-make sport, as much as he said people tried to trick the game up and complicate it and use all those analytics numbers you heard the announcers talking about on television. Right now the Griz were making their shots.

And the Hawks were missing theirs.

Bakari was already three for three. Wes didn't make any of

them easy for him, crowding him as much as he could without getting whistled for fouls. Didn't matter. Bakari was still three for three. Wes missed his first two shots. Dinero missed his first two shots. It was 10–0 for the Grizzlies before E beat Trevor Arrazi to a Russ Adams miss, and got an easy putback.

Wes thought Coach might call an early timeout, just to get everybody settled down. But he decided to let the Hawks play their way out of their early funk, and into the championship game.

At 12–2, Dinero almost ordered Wes to take the Hawks' next shot even without saying a word. He threw the ball to Wes in the right corner, and Wes had some daylight. But he kept thinking about the two shots he'd already missed. Passed it back to Dinero. Ran to the left corner. Dinero dribbled over to that side. Passed him the ball again.

A little more daylight this time.

Okay, Wes thought to himself, almost as if Dinero could hear him.

Okay.

Bakari ran at him. Wes put a neat up-fake on him, took two dribbles to his right, put up a jumper.

All net.

"You better keep doing that," Dinero said as they got back on defense. "'Cause I'm gonna keep feeding you."

Wes just nodded.

Okay.

By the end of the quarter they had cut the Grizzlies' lead to a basket. By halftime the Hawks were playing like the team that had rolled into the tournament with just one loss. They were back in rhythm. They were rolling. And ahead by six.

The only problem was that both Wes and Dinero picked up their second fouls with two minutes left in the half, on back-to-back plays. Wes fouled Bakari on a drive. Dinero got called for an offensive foul, knocking over Tate Brooks on a drive of his own.

Coach got them both out of there. As they were getting ready to start the third quarter, he pulled both Wes and Dinero aside.

"I want you both to keep playing your games, and stay aggressive," he said. "But if either one of you picks up a third, I got to sit you down. Got it?"

"We both do," Dinero said.

The third quarter turned out to be the best ball, from both teams, the Hawks and Grizzlies had played against each other, the first two games and now this one. Both teams were running every chance they could. Both teams were pressing. Both teams were knocking down good shots, starting with their best players: Wes, Dinero, Bakari, Tate.

We're *all* exactly where we're supposed to be, Wes told himself.

Wes did pick up his third foul, with thirty seconds left in the quarter. But Coach left him in for the Hawks' last possession. Wes told himself to be careful and stay away from contact.

Only with five seconds left, he got a step on Bakari, saw a lane to the basket, and took off. At the last second, Trevor Arrazi left E and jumped out on him. Wes thought there was no doubt that Trevor had gotten there late, hadn't established his position when they collided.

Wes made the shot. Heard the whistle. Had to be a chance

for a three-point play. Had to be a foul on Trevor. But when he turned around, he saw the ref closest to the play pointing at Wes with his left hand, patting the back of his head with his right.

"That's a charge, Number Thirteen," he said.

Fourth foul.

With the whole fourth quarter left to play.

FORTY-FIVE

DINERO PICKED UP HIS THIRD foul with seven minutes left in the game, but Wes knew he wasn't coming out, not with Wes still seated next to Coach Saunders.

It was 40–40 by then.

The Hawks were hanging in, even with Wes out of the game. Casey Fisher was guarding Bakari and it was clear that Casey didn't give a rip about scoring himself, as long as he could hold down Bakari.

Which he was doing.

Wes didn't ask Coach when he could go back in. He'd never asked one of his coaches a question like that in his life. Just trusted that Coach would know when the time was right.

At one point Wes turned around and looked at his dad, who put up both hands, his way of telling Wes to relax.

Easy for him to say.

It was 48–47, Grizzlies, three minutes left, when Coach turned to Wes and said, "Okay, son. Go help win us this game."

"Gonna try," Wes said.

"Can't do it if you foul out," Coach said. "So try real hard not to do *that*."

A minute later Wes hit a three to put the Hawks ahead by a basket. The Griz surprised the Hawks and tried to fast break even after a made basket. Bakari inbounded the ball to Tate at half-court. Wes stayed with Bakari, but could see Tate breaking away from Dinero, on his way to the basket, Dinero chasing after him as if trying to catch him and pass him in a running race.

Don't foul, Wes thought.

Hoping that Dinero was thinking the same thing.

As Tate elevated, Dinero reached in, and seemed to have made a great play, knocked the ball away cleanly.

Unfortunately, the ref didn't see it that way.

He called Dinero for *his* fourth foul. Wes could see, even from a distance, Dinero thought he'd gotten a bad whistle. *Really* bad whistle. But he knew enough not to say anything that could get him a technical foul, and potentially make this a four-point play for the Griz.

So Tate only got two free throws.

Made them both.

Game tied again.

Wes made a jumper, just inside the free-throw line, at the other end. Hawks by two. Bakari threw up a wild shot to beat the shot clock, nearly falling down as he did.

Somehow he banked the sucker home.

Game tied again.

Under a minute left in the championship game.

Dinero got loose from Tate, put up one of his soft, sweet tear-drop shots. But somehow it rolled off the side of the rim. The Grizzlies pushed again, thinking they could get a quick shot, put themselves into a two-for-one situation if they could score before there were thirty-five seconds left.

Wes guarded Bakari as closely as he could dare. Bakari rushed his shot, banged it off the front of the rim. E looked as if he had the rebound, but Trevor knocked the ball away from him.

The ball bounced away from everybody, toward midcourt.

Wes chased. And Bakari. And Tate Brooks. And Dinero, trailing the other three by a couple of steps.

Somehow they all dove for the ball at once, as if the championship were on the floor in front of them.

Dinero was the last one to the party, as Wes and Bakari wrestled to gain control of the ball.

They all heard the whistle then.

All turned and saw the taller of the two refs with his hand already in there, ready to make a foul call.

All four players froze. The ref hesitated, as if he couldn't decide who in the scramble of bodies in front of him had actually committed a foul.

That's when Dinero jumped up, slapped the front of his jersey in frustration as if he couldn't believe what he'd just done, and raised his hand in the air.

As soon as Dinero did, the ref nodded, pointed at him, and called Dinero for his fifth foul. He was out of the game. As he walked past Wes, on his way to the Hawks' bench, Dinero said, "Win this for us. For all of us."

Then he smiled.

Josh walked up to the scorer's table to replace Dinero. Wes watched as Dinero walked with him, saying something into his ear, Josh nodding as he did. Coach quickly gathered the Hawks around him. Bakari was on his way to the free-throw line. The ref had decided he was the one who had gotten fouled, and awarded him a one-and-one.

"Whether he makes both or not, no timeout," Coach said. "Push the ball and get them backing up. Somebody will get open. Just make sure there's enough time for us to get a rebound and a put-back if we miss."

Bakari made the first free throw. Missed the second. E got the rebound and passed the ball to Josh. Thirty seconds left. Hawks down by a point.

E came up, looking for a possible pick-and-roll.

Nothing.

Wes was over on the right wing, on his way to go get the ball, when he heard this:

"Josh."

It was Dinero's voice.

Wes looked at Josh. He was dribbling with his right hand. But dropped his left hand to his side as he looked back at Wes.

And made the money gesture with his fingers.

In that moment, it was like Wes was back in his driveway with Dinero.

He took a step toward half-court, then made the back-door cut his dad had been teaching him his whole life.

Josh threw him a perfect pass, like the one the boy Danny had thrown in Mr. C's game.

Wes caught it, had room for one dribble, laid the ball home.

Hawks by a point.

But the game wasn't over. As soon as Wes scored, he was running back on defense, running hard to find Bakari, which is why he was in position to intercept Tate's pass for Bakari as the clock ran out and the Hawks won the championship.

Dinero got to him first.

"Money," he said to Wes.

FORTY-SIX

THERE WAS ONE LAST FIGHT between Wes and Dinero.

The championship bowl had already been presented to Coach Saunders and the Hawks. After that it was time for the chairman of the board for the league, Bakari's dad, to announce who would get the trophy as MVP of the championship game.

When Mr. Hogan announced it was Wes who'd been voted MVP by the board members, Wes immediately tried to hand the trophy to Dinero.

Dinero handed it right back.

Wes handed it to him again.

Dinero handed it back.

By then, all of their teammates were laughing. So was Coach.

"Don't try to get one more assist, Thirteen," Dinero said. "Josh already got the one that mattered."

"Thanks to you," Josh said.

Wes looked at Dinero and made the money gesture with his own fingers now. Dinero did the same. Then all of the Hawks were doing it.

Finally Wes walked over to where his dad was standing with his arm around Wes's mom.

"Well now," Lt. Michael Davies said. "Where should we go to celebrate?"

"Where do you guys want to go?" he said to his parents.

In the same moment, they said, "Home."

And they did.